Tales of the Were
Grizzly Cove

Badass Bear

BIANCA D'ARC

This book is a work of fiction. The names, characters, places, and incidents are products of the writer's imagination or have been used fictitiously and are not to be construed as real. Any resemblance to persons, living or dead, actual events, locale or organizations is entirely coincidental.

No part of this book may be used or reproduced in any manner whatsoever without written permission, except in the case of brief quotations embodied in critical articles and reviews.

DEDICATION

To my friends and family. Thanks to Peggy McChesney, who helps spot typos and oopsies like nobody's business.

And I'd like to dedicate this book to my mother, who watches over me and the family from above nowadays. I hope she's watching now...and always.

CHAPTER ONE

Trevor Williams, former Army Ranger and current high-level intelligence operative for the band of mercenaries that had gathered under Major Jesse Moore on his Wyoming mountaintop, was back in Grizzly Cove, Washington. He'd visited briefly a couple of weeks ago to talk with an Australian koala shifter—of all things—who had been held prisoner in the mountains of Oregon for months.

The hunt was still on for those who had been holding the koala-man and several other shifters in a private menagerie. Trevor's unit had found evidence of medical experiments having been performed on the captive shifters, among other atrocities. The mercenary unit was still actively searching the mountains in and around Oregon for any sign of the bastards that had kidnapped and imprisoned so many. Trevor's job was to liaise with the shifters who had settled in Grizzly Cove and, secondarily, try to get more intel on the mer shifters that had recently moved into the waters of the cove, using it as a sanctuary.

Major Moore—as well as their employer on this particular job, the billionaire lion Alpha, Samson Kinkaid—wanted as much information as possible on the threat in the ocean and any possible allies they might be able to claim. Trevor was an expert at gathering intelligence, and the bear shifters who had set up Grizzly Cove knew it. Trev was under no illusion that John Marshall, Alpha of this band of bears, didn't know exactly why Trevor was there.

But he respected Big John and the men he'd gathered around him. They were all veterans of various branches of the Special Forces, and they had recently retired to civilian life. That they'd set up a town all their own was pretty remarkable. Then again, this unit of shifters had always been kind of remarkable.

Most of them were bears of one kind or other. Many were grizzlies, but there were a few black bears, even a polar bear, along with a few other, rarer bears. All were former soldiers, and they'd worked together for years, forming a tight family of men who trusted each other without question or comment.

Trevor had worked with them a time or two, but he'd been part of a different unit, and he was a bit younger than the core group that had settled Grizzly Cove. He respected them all, but they'd run in slightly different circles while in the military. Still, he liked what he'd seen of what they'd built here, on the rugged coast of Washington State, and he almost wished he'd been closer with them so he could claim one of the plots of land around the cove and build himself a place to settle down.

He liked Wyoming well enough, but something about the ocean had always drawn him. And the salmon in this part of the world were some of the juiciest, which appealed to his wilder half. His inner grizzly loved good sushi.

So, while his comrades were in full search mode in Oregon and beyond, Trevor had been assigned—with Big John's permission—to liaise with Grizzly Cove and its inhabitants. The koala shifter who had been held prisoner was still here, now mated to a selkie shifter from Kinkaid's Clan. Apparently, she'd been sent to gather information on the cove's businesses and social order, and had been lucky enough to find her mate in the process.

For now, she was still part of the Kinkaid mega-corporation and hierarchy, but Trevor had been told she was also a woman on her honeymoon. Samson Kinkaid had given her a month off from work so she could enjoy her honeymoon with her new mate before getting back to business matters.

Which was where Trevor came in. Kinkaid had hired Trevor's unit to hunt down those who were still missing from the menagerie, especially a lion shifter female who had last been seen injured badly in the woods of Oregon. They'd found her trail, but she was very good at hiding and had not yet been found.

Kinkaid wanted those who had held the shifters captive, and he had deep enough pockets to keep the search going for a very long time, indeed. Samson Kinkaid was a billionaire with business interests all over the world. He could afford to pay Trevor's expenses, and he had asked that Trevor take over as Kinkaid's eyes and ears in the cove.

He was happy enough to do it. Being in Grizzly Cove wasn't a tough assignment—not by a long shot. Not one to sit around doing nothing all day, Trevor had agreed to pitch in and help with some of the construction work that was going on all over town. He worked a few days a week, making friends and renewing old ties, which helped him with his primary task of gathering intel. It was hard to learn things if you didn't speak to people, and it was hard to make friends with people who were busy trying to keep up with a building boom.

The arrival of the mer in the cove had spurred a construction spike as new accommodations were designed and added to the town's growing infrastructure. The new boathouse was already up and running, as an example. The complex structure had been built first because it was where water-based shifters could enter and leave the cove without being seen by anyone. There was a water entrance below the building, which was built half on a pier that extended over the cove. There were locker rooms and showers where the water shifters could clean up and dress or undress, as the case may be.

Trev had just finished work for the day and was heading down Main Street on his way to the half-finished hotel where he was currently bunking down. It wasn't perfect, but his room was fully equipped and the rest of the building was coming along. He got a nice discount on his lodgings because he was bartering carpentry skills in the evenings, helping the proprietor put the finishing touches on all the guest rooms. Trevor was particularly good with plaster and drywall, but he had all-around carpentry training from when he'd been a youngster, working with his father's small specialty plaster business. His dad had been a true artist, and he'd taught his son everything he knew.

The hotel was on the other end of town from the jobsite Trevor had been working on today, but the weather was cool and pleasant, and the sun was shining. It was a nice walk along the road that hugged the shore of the cove closest at this point.

He was thinking about where he might

get dinner tonight when he heard a sound that immediately caught his attention. Looking for the source, he spotted a woman sitting on a rock down by the shore. And she was crying.

It was her muffled sobs he'd heard, carried to him on the fickle breeze.

The way she was sitting reminded him of the statue in Copenhagen he'd seen once. The little mermaid, he thought it was called, and it depicted a mermaid sitting on a rock, just the way this woman was sitting. Though she wore clothing and he could see legs in place of a tail, mer were so prevalent in Grizzly Cove right now that it was a pretty safe bet that she was a mermaid—wearing her human form at the moment.

Her soft crying got to him, though. He couldn't just walk past and leave her in such a state. He wasn't sure exactly what he could do to help her, but he would do his best to try. Squaring his shoulders, Trevor stepped off the sidewalk and headed down to the water's edge.

Beth hated it here. Ever since they'd come to Grizzly Cove, her whole life had been turned upside down. She'd loved being part of the hunting party, but that was all over now. Three of the other girls had mated with bears, and the hunting party had just been dissolved.

Besides, the ocean wasn't safe for hunting at the moment, anyway. Nobody was going out beyond the magical barrier that kept the leviathan and its minions out of the cove. The mer were settling in and making a new home here in the cove, and Beth truly felt like a fish out of water. She didn't like it here. She didn't like change, and she especially didn't like the bears. They were scary, and her friends—or the women she'd thought were her friends—were turning their backs on her to be with their bear shifter mates.

Nansee, the leader of their pod, had just given Beth the news. Her hunting party was no more, and, in fact, nobody was going out hunting in the sea until the leviathan was dealt with once and for all. If she still wanted to serve, she could do so by patrolling the mouth of the cove, just on this side of the magical ward that kept the evil creature out.

But that was boring. Beth would do it, but it wasn't like hunting with the others, where she'd been learning new skills—

especially how to protect herself. She'd been the newest member of the team, with the most to learn, but she hadn't minded. She liked learning about how to use the weapons of their trade. Especially the knives. Those skills would work on land or in the water, and it had helped her feel more confident about her personal safety.

The other girls wouldn't teach her now. Not the mated ones, anyway. Maybe Janice and Marla might still be persuaded to show her a few things while they patrolled the ward, but the others were living on land with their new mates and only swam for fun, not for work.

The simple fact was…she missed them. She felt too vulnerable on land and didn't want to be here, but the ocean wasn't safe anymore. Her safe place had been overrun by evil creatures. Kind of like life on land, to her way of thinking.

She heard the crunch of footsteps on the rocky sand, and then, a shadow fell over her. Adrenaline poured through her system as she palmed one of the knives she was never without nowadays and looked up at the man who had snuck up on her.

"Mind if I join you?"

His voice was deep and melodic. It soothed her raw nerves just the tiniest bit, but she knew to be wary of men on land. The sun was behind him, so all she really got was the impression of massive shoulders on a tall, muscular frame. He must be one of the bears, then. Why couldn't they just leave her alone?

She couldn't speak, her heart still in her throat, so she couldn't tell him to go away. He seemed to take her silence as agreement and lowered himself to the rocky beach a few feet away. He looked relaxed and comfortable, sitting facing the water with his elbows resting on his raised knees. He didn't look directly at her again, which lowered her heart rate a bit more. Instead, he stared out at the waters of the cove and the ocean beyond.

"I'm sorry if I startled you," he went on as if they were having a conversation. His voice was gentle, and her taut nerves slowly quieted.

She was ashamed to admit she'd frozen in place when he'd started talking. At least she'd armed herself, but if she couldn't move due to fright, what good would her little knife do? Misery mixed with the fear still coursed through her blood.

"My name is Trevor. I'm new in town, but I've known the guys who run this place a while. We served around the same time, though I'm a slightly younger vintage than Big John and the others," he went on.

Why was he talking to her? She wasn't responding—that simple feat was still beyond her at the moment, overrun with nerves as she was. So why did he continue speaking?

"I didn't mean to frighten you," he said, and she cringed. Of course. He was a bear with a sensitive nose. He could probably smell her fear. Great. "I just wanted to see if there was anything I could do to help. I heard you sniffle, and a fellow can't just walk past when a beautiful girl is so upset that she's staring out at the ocean, crying." His voice dipped even lower. "Do you miss being out at sea that much?"

His words made her turn her head to look at him. He really was a handsome man, if you weren't afraid of big, muscular guys with combat skills and a ferocious animal side.

"I don't miss the ocean as much as I miss my hunting party," she admitted, surprising herself by speaking the words. What had come over her? She didn't want to get chummy with a bear.

"Ah. You're a huntress. I think I understand. You want to be out there, fighting the leviathan instead of cowering behind the ward." He was nodding as if he had uncovered some secret of the universe.

"You couldn't be more wrong," she told him, wanting to bring him down a peg. "I miss my old life. The girls were teaching me so much, and now, my hunting party is gone because three of my so-called friends mated your kind." She must be feeling stronger because, that time, even she heard the disdain in her words. Good. Let the bear know he wasn't welcome. Maybe then he'd go away.

"So it seems everything isn't as rosy as they paint it here in Grizzly Cove," he said unexpectedly, making her look at him with suspicion. "I'd been told everyone was happy with the new arrangement." He nodded toward the water. "The mer in the cove and the bears on the shore. I thought maybe it was all too good to be true."

She eyed his work clothes and the sawdust that clung to his jeans. "But you're one of them. You've obviously been building things."

His eyebrows rose, and he looked down at his legs, brushing at the clinging bits of wood shavings. "Observant as well as pretty," he said offhandedly, and somehow, his words made her blush. Silly human skin, showing every little emotion, no matter how out of place. "I'm not really *one of them*, as you put it. I'm based out of Wyoming at the moment, and I'm under contract to the Kinkaid Alpha to act as liaison with the folks here for a bit."

"Kinkaid? But that Clan is full of lions and selkies," she blurted, not censoring her thoughts at all. "I thought you were a bear. Are you a lion?" She hated the way her voice trembled with fear as she stared at him. The nerves were coming back in full force. Bears were bad enough, but lions? She didn't think she could handle meeting a lion shifter.

"No, sweetheart. You were right. I'm a bear, not a cat. I'm just working on behalf of the lion Alpha because my commander thought I'd fit in better with the folks here. We have the beast in common, plus, like I said, I worked with most of the core group in the past."

"Commander? Are you still in the military?" she asked, despite her desire to end this conversation as quickly as possible.

"No. I've gone private. I work for a group that helps other shifters—for a price—when they need specialists."

His explanation seemed harmless enough until she remembered…

"The Wraiths?" Her voice rose in pitch as alarm filled her. "You're one of the *Wraiths?*"

He surprised her by chuckling. "I never liked that nickname. We just call ourselves Moore's men, because we all work for Major Moore and live on his mountain in Wyoming."

"But…" She was shocked he'd admit to it so readily. "The Wraiths are said to walk like phantoms, and they punish shifters who cross them."

He laughed harder this time. "The only people we punish are those who deserve it. And if we move quietly, that's because we train hard to keep up our stealth skills. I'm glad to see our legend is growing though. Where did you hear all that?"

"Jonathan said—" She stopped herself from saying any more. She shouldn't have even uttered his name. Doing that might conjure him up, and that was the last thing she wanted. Ever.

"Who's Jonathan?" the bear asked, but she turned away. She had already said far too much.

She wanted to jump into the water and swim away, but she couldn't. Even here, she had to use the boathouse's secret entrance to the water to hide her true form and abilities. They couldn't risk being seen, and while there wasn't much traffic on the road through Grizzly Cove yet, it was still a public thoroughfare, open to humans. Everyone in town knew they had to shift with the utmost discretion. They couldn't afford strange tales of mermaids or werebears getting around and drawing a crowd of curious humans to the town.

She stood abruptly, half-fearing the Wraith would follow, but he made no move to stand. It was small comfort though, since the Wraiths were said to have uncommon speed and deadly skill. He could probably kill her in the blink of an eye…or worse.

"I've got to go," she whispered, hoping against hope that he would let her. The adrenaline pushed her to walk away, and she managed a few feet before breaking into a run.

CHAPTER TWO

Trevor scratched his head as he watched the young mermaid run from him. He hadn't meant to scare the poor girl out of her wits. He'd just wanted to offer some comfort. Instead, he'd made things worse.

He knew enough not to make a move until she was out of sight. A frightened creature didn't need to think it was being chased. Any move on his part would have made her panic worse, though it went against his nature to let her go in such a state. If only there was something he could do to help her.

"Don't take it personally," a female voice said from farther down the beach. She was speaking quietly, but she must've known he could hear her even from such a distance.

She was walking with a man he recognized from his Army days. Trevor had heard Jack Chambers had found his mate, but he hadn't realized he'd mated a mermaid. Trevor stood as they approached, and he saw the look of concern on the woman's face as he shook hands with Jack. They hadn't seen each other in years, but at one time, they'd been good friends.

"This is Grace," Jack introduced the woman at his side. Trevor smiled at her, genuinely happy for his friend.

"Congratulations on your mating," he said to both of them.

"Thanks," Grace said, smiling faintly in return. "About Beth..." Trevor surmised Beth must be the woman who had fled. "She was the newest member of my hunting party, and she's taking the move to the cove very hard."

"It seems like more than that, I'm afraid. She was in a panic when she found out who I work for."

Grace seemed confused, but her mate clarified.

"You've heard me talk about the

mercenary group under Major Moore. Trevor is one of his guys. Is intelligence gathering still your thing, Trev?" Jack asked. Only with his former comrades would Trevor be so open about who he was and what he did. He nodded in agreement.

"Wait a minute. I never connected it before, but that mercenary group in Wyoming. They're called the Wraiths, aren't they?" Grace asked, realization dawning on her pretty face.

"Some call us that," Trevor admitted. "I've never much liked that name myself."

"You may not know this, but some mer scare their children with threats of the Wraiths," Grace told them, frowning. "I think it started as an old folk tale, and then, when a real group of fighting men took that name, the legend just sprouted fins and swam wild."

It took Trevor a moment to process the aquatic wording, but he got the gist of what she was saying. His unit's existence had gotten tied up with some old wives' tale, and now, they'd become the threat mer parents used to keep their children in line. No wonder Beth had freaked out and run.

"Just to be clear, we didn't choose that

name. It was laid upon us," Trevor told them. "But the rest of the guys seemed to like it, so the major didn't object."

"Well, the legend seems to have grown," Jack commented.

"Beth mentioned someone named Jonathan," Trev put out there to see what kind of response he'd get. Jack's expression didn't change, but his mate frowned, anger sparking in her eyes.

"Jonathan is a shark," was all she said at first.

"A bad guy, eh?" Trevor prompted.

"No. He's really a shark." Her words surprised him and her mate both, judging by Jack's startled expression and the way he focused on her words. "There aren't many that we know of, but we have crossed paths with a handful of shark shifters in the oceans, and on land. Mostly, they keep to themselves, but Jonathan is a right bastard. Beth's mother lives with him. Whether it's of her own accord or not, nobody can say. All I know is, Beth ran away from home and sought refuge in our pod. Nansee went to bat for her, and there was a rather tense standoff for a while before Jonathan seemed to give up and leave Beth to us. Her mother is still with him, though, and I don't think Beth has had any contact with her since she left. I don't think Jonathan would allow it."

"Do you know his last name? Or where he lives?" Trevor asked, mindful of including this intel in his next report to Moore and Kinkaid. The lion Alpha probably already knew about there being such a thing as a shark shifter since he was related to so many selkies, but Trevor was pretty sure Moore was as clueless as Trevor had been about their existence.

"Chase," Grace replied. "Jonathan Chase. He has a mansion on Catalina Island. It's at the southern end of our pod's range, but we winter in the area, and that's when Beth escaped and sought sanctuary with us."

"A mansion?" Jack asked his mate.

"I said he was a shark. I mean that in every sense of the word." Grace made a stern face. "He has some kind of import-export business, and he's rich. He's also a mean bastard who traumatized Beth. She doesn't talk about it, but it's easy to see she's afraid of powerful men. I think that's why she's had such a hard time getting used to living here. The bears intimidate her, though she'll never admit it."

Trevor felt awful. He should have just walked past and left the poor girl in peace. Yet…he couldn't have done that. It wasn't in his nature to not stop and help someone in distress. And if he hadn't stopped, he never would have learned all this interesting information about shark shifters. So, in essence, he wouldn't have been doing his job if he hadn't used the opportunity to gather intel.

Which only made him feel worse. Beth's pain wasn't part of his job. He hadn't meant to cause her so much anxiety and outright fear. He felt like a creep.

He had to find some way to apologize to her and make her see that not all men were rat bastards like this shark fellow, Jonathan Chase. Of course, Trevor might just need some sort of miracle to get close to her again. She'd probably run the other way if she saw him coming down the street after their recent encounter.

"Well. I'd better go clean up," Trevor said, realizing he still hadn't made it back to the hotel for the hot shower he'd wanted after spending all day working.

"Do you have any plans for dinner?" Grace asked unexpectedly.

Trevor shook his head. "No. I was just going to grab a sandwich or something after I hit the shower."

"Oh, I think we can do better than that for you," Grace replied, looking at her mate and back again. "Why don't you come to dinner at our place? Nothing formal, just old friends sharing a meal. I'm sure Jack would like a chance to catch up with you. Right, Jack?"

Her mate nodded, smiling at the idea. "Yeah, that'd be great. What do you say, Trev? Meet us back at our place after you get a chance to clean up?"

"If you're sure. I wouldn't want you to go to any trouble," Trevor said politely.

Grace replied for them both, assuring Trevor that they'd be overjoyed to have him as their guest. The timing was set and arrangements finalized. Jack gave Trevor directions to their place, and then, they parted with promises to see each other again in a couple of hours.

*

Trevor found the house with no problem. As he approached, he noted the surveillance gizmos in the bushes. They were well-hidden, but not well enough for a pro like him not to spot at least some of them. Good. Jack hadn't lost his edge since quitting the service. With a new mate to protect, he'd probably beefed up security. Heaven knows, that's what Trevor would do if he was ever blessed to find his mate and have a permanent home with her.

All the same, Trevor waved at one of the cameras, just so Jack would know that Trev was still on his game. Later, when Jack reviewed the tapes, he'd have a laugh. Then, if he was as thorough as he had been in the service, he'd go out and move that particular camera to a less obvious spot.

When Trevor mounted the wooden steps that led to the front door, it was opened. Jack stood just inside, a broad smile on his face and the soft tones of feminine conversation wafting from within the house. More than just his mate was in there.

"I thought it only fair to warn you, Grace decided to meddle. Beth's in there. She'll be joining us for dinner," Jack said before Trevor could say a word.

He paused on the top step, then continued forward. "Good. I wanted a chance to apologize to her."

"Just tread carefully," Jack advised. "And don't expect too much. Beth barely tolerates me, and Grace and I have been together the longest out of her mated friends."

"I hear you," Trevor agreed, handing the bottle of wine he'd brought to Jack.

The dinner that followed was both delicious and filling. It was a surf and turf, appropriately. Grace kept the conversation flowing, though Beth was a bit subdued. Slowly, she seemed to get used to having Trevor seated across from her—especially when Jack brought up some of the non-classified stories about their time serving together.

After dinner, they retired to the deck, which had a great view of the ocean and the mouth of the cove. Jack and Grace had shooed Trevor and Beth outside, promising drinks after they did a quick cleanup of the table. Both Trevor and Beth had offered to help and had been politely, but firmly, refused.

"So, does the ward extend straight across the mouth of the cove?" Trevor asked as they looked out at the water. From this vantage point, they had quite a view.

"More or less," Beth said. She'd warmed up to him enough during dinner to allow for somewhat easier conversation. "It bows in a few degrees at the apex, but those who know more about magic than I do say that's to be expected."

"When you're in the water, what does the ward feel like? I mean, do you know when you're getting close to the edge?" Trevor asked more factual questions to keep her talking and, hopefully, extend the easy camaraderie that was developing between them.

"Yeah, it's pretty obvious. Even I can feel it, and I'm not really that open to sensing magic—or so I've been told. The water feels kind of…thick, I guess I would say. And you can see the creatures out beyond the barrier just waiting for someone foolish enough to swim out too far. They're just awful."

"So, the enemy is patrolling the other side, just like your people are keeping watch on our side?"

"There are a lot more of them than us," Beth said candidly. "We have patrols, but they have an army right up against the barrier. It's scary. If the ward ever fell, it would be disaster."

26

"Except, you could swim for land, right? Most, if not all, of your pod could make it out of the water in case of a breach. At least, that's what Big John told me when I asked him," Trevor admitted.

He was feeling her out. Maybe he could work with her. Maybe that would be a way to put her a little more at ease around him. Or not. Either way, he still had a job to do, and she might just be able to help him do it.

"You've been asking the bears about us?" Beth asked, looking at him with suspicion.

Honesty was called for here, he knew. "It's part of my job. I'm trying to get a feel for the place and a sense of the safety parameters for all the inhabitants. I was sent here to observe and report back to my commander and, ultimately, the Kinkaid Alpha, who's paying the bills, but the information doesn't have to flow just one way. I'm fully authorized to help out and offer advice if I think I can improve the situation here. The lion Alpha is very familiar—more familiar than I am—with water-based shifters because of all the selkies in his Clan. He has an interest in helping keep the oceans free of the leviathan menace, and aside from all that, he's a decent guy. He doesn't want to see innocents suffer."

"But he's a lion." Beth looked as if she wanted to recall her words the moment they were out of her mouth.

It seemed she had a real problem with apex predators, and you couldn't really get any higher up the food chain than the lion king himself. Of course, bears were just as ferocious, but they kept a lower profile as a general rule. The question was...how did he put Beth's mind at ease about what must be a bunch of scary shifters all around her?

Then, a thought occurred to him. "Have you spoken with Moira Kinkaid?"

"The selkie?" Beth asked, frowning. "I've seen her swimming around a bit, but she's newly mated and spends most of her time on land with Seamus."

"You know Seamus?"

Beth's voice didn't hold the same fear when she mentioned the koala shifter's name. He was the one and only koala in Grizzly Cove, having been abducted from his homeland of Australia. When he escaped the menagerie, he'd found his way to Grizzly Cove and had been something of the town drunk for a while...until he'd met Moira. He was sober as a judge these days and gave every indication of being a truly happy man.

"Until recently, it was hard to avoid him. He was always passing out on the beach, and the other girls used to move him farther ashore when the incoming tide threatened to drown him. We were all told to watch out for him. They said he'd been held prisoner and we should feel sorry for him."

It was hard to tell from the tone of her voice whether Beth actually did feel sorry for Seamus or was too wrapped up in her own misery to have sympathy for anyone else. Trevor shook his head. He wasn't sure how to reach someone who was so inwardly focused. Still, he had to try. He couldn't leave her like this—scared of everything and acting out in a negative way.

"Seamus had a rough road getting here," Trevor admitted. "I was on the team that discovered the menagerie where he'd been held for months in his animal form. It was pretty terrible. There was evidence that whoever was holding him—and several other shifters—was conducting some sort of medical experiments on them."

"That's awful!"

Finally, she was reacting in the way he

would expect of any decent being. Maybe he was getting through to her with a few hard facts.

"Yeah, it was bad. Some of the worst I've seen, and I've been around the world, to a lot of hellish places. I've seen bad stuff before, and this was right up there with the baddest of the bad. Thing is, he's doing a lot better now that he's found his mate, and Moira is someone you should get to know if you really want to know what the Kinkaid Alpha is like. She's his cousin, you know."

Beth's expression held genuine astonishment. "You're kidding."

"I'm not. The Kinkaid Clan is ruled by a lion, but there are many selkies in the Clan, as well. Their roots go back to both Ireland and Africa, and through a quirky twist of fate, Samson Kinkaid ended up the king of all lions. It's not something he was born into, from what I understand. He was happy enough building his own little empire here in the States with his somewhat eccentric Clan, but when the leader of all lions in Africa was killed, along with all logical successors, the title fell to Samson—or so the legend goes." Trevor shifted his stance, hoping to appear non-threatening, though he knew that was a lot to ask given his size. "I've met him a few times, you know. He's a pretty nice guy, and he really cares for his people."

"But lions eat their young," Beth whispered, shocking a laugh out of Trevor.

"Oh, honey. No. Just no." He chuckled. "Samson Kinkaid is a caring Alpha. He's more likely to harm himself than anyone who comes under his protection, from the smallest cub to the frailest elder."

"Anybody for wine?" Grace asked as she walked out onto the deck, holding a bottle and a glass. Her mate followed close behind with more glasses for the rest of them.

Trevor felt he'd made some progress with Beth, but he had just one more thing to say before they rejoined the other couple. "Talk to Moira."

Beth's nose scrunched up adorably as she seemed to think about his words. Finally, she nodded once, decisively. "I will."

They walked away from the rail, toward the patio table where the Grace and her mate were already pouring glasses of the wine Trevor had brought with him. It was a slightly sweet wine of good vintage from Maxwell's world famous vineyard, perfect for relaxing after dinner.

31

*

A few days after the dinner at Grace and Jack's house, Trevor was once again heading back to his room after a hard day's work at the construction site. And once again, he spotted Beth sitting on that rock she seemed to favor. He'd just been thinking about how little he'd accomplished in the days since talking to Beth. The report he'd filed right after the dinner had been full of the information she'd provided about the ward and its limitations.

He was due to file another report in a few days, and he wasn't sure what he was going to put in it. He'd been so busy helping the other bears build on to their town, he hadn't had much time to really question anybody, or learn anything new. That was a problem. A big problem.

Working construction wasn't why Trevor had been sent to Grizzly Cove. Oh, he was all for helping the guys build stuff while he was in town, but his primary focus—and his *paying* job—had to be gathering intelligence. Recon was his thing, and in the past few days, he hadn't been doing much, if any, true reconnaissance. That had to change. Soon.

Since she'd been so helpful before, Trevor thought maybe he should try again with Beth. From what he could see as he approached her rock slowly, at least she wasn't crying this time. She looked...wistful, he thought. Not really sad, but not really happy either. He figured that had to be better than tears, right?

"Hi, Beth," he said quietly, hoping to avoid startling her.

It didn't work. She still jumped, but settled down when she turned her head and saw him. That was some progress, at least.

"Hi, Trevor. Been sawing things again?" She nodded toward his dusty jeans where bits of sawdust clung no matter what he did. Of course, he wasn't much of a fashion plate, and a little sawdust didn't really bother him.

"Yep. Sawing. Framing. Nailing. You name it." If she'd been any other woman, he might've thrown in some silly double entendre about *screwing* too, but Beth would probably run away from him, as fast as her little feet—or fins—could carry her.

CHAPTER THREE

Trevor had caught her off guard. Again. But this time, she didn't really mind so much. Odd, that. Somehow, after spending an evening with him and her friend, Grace and her new mate, Trevor didn't seem quite so scary anymore.

In fact, after taking his advice and talking with the selkie, Moira, Beth found that she was losing some of her fear of the big apex predators. Oh, she figured she would always be wary around some of them, but she'd at least learned that a few of the really frightening guys in Grizzly Cove weren't quite as barbaric as she'd always believed them to be.

Jack was one that had won her over. The way he treated Grace—with obvious love and affection—was clear to see. He seemed to really be making an effort with the rest of their old hunting party, including Beth. She hadn't expected that. After all, she hadn't been very nice to him and the other bears since coming here.

She was making an effort to modify her own behavior. She wasn't very proud of the way she'd conducted herself to this point. She had a bit of apologizing to do, and a lot of humble pie to eat. Luckily, the ladies who ran the bakery were very understanding. Beth had started there, trying to erase her earlier snide remarks and bad behavior by actually spending time in the shop, eating there, instead of taking her order to go and running away.

She had been there when the sisters' mates had shown up a few times now, and she'd done her best to be, if not *friendly*, at least not as rude as she had been before. They'd seemed to respond well to her change in attitude, but it was early days yet. She had to go slowly because the fear of those big, powerful men hadn't totally left her.

Oh, she knew intellectually that they were mated to humans. That meant something significant in itself. Those formidable men had tempered their strength in order to be with their fragile human mates. If they could do that—and the evidence of their mates' happiness and continued good health meant they could—then perhaps, they weren't as ferocious as she had always been led to believe.

"You might be interested to know, I did as you suggested and had a talk with Moira. She's very nice, and yes, you were right…" Beth smiled and rolled her eyes to inject some humor into her words. "Moira is already halfway to convincing me that her cousin isn't as bad as I thought he was. She's even invited me to dinner once she and Seamus get their house in order. They only moved in yesterday, so everything is in disarray. I helped her do a bit of unpacking in the kitchen while we chatted."

That innocent domestic chore of unwrapping dishes and putting them in cupboards had been fun. It was one of the very few times in her life when Beth had been in her human form and not afraid of anything or anyone. Moira was easy to like and a fellow water shifter, even if she was a seal and not a mer.

They'd hit it off, talking about the advantages of living in the cove rather than the open sea. And Moira was mated to Seamus—a cuddly little koala bear shifter, not a giant, angry grizzly bear. Even though he was male, his thick Aussie accent and his animal side didn't make Beth apprehensive. On the contrary, she felt welcomed by them both, and as if she had made two new friends.

Beth never took to people that easily. Not even her fellow mer. Then again, she hadn't really been as open before. She'd come a long way from the shy runaway she had been only a few years ago. Oh, she was still shy, and scared of a lot, but she was getting bolder each day, with each new experience, and she thought maybe she'd had a bit of a personal growth spurt since coming to Grizzly Cove, and especially since meeting Trevor.

"I'm glad," Trevor said, and Beth had to backtrack in her mind to figure out what he was responding to. "Everything I've seen of Moira, and her cousin, leads me to believe that the Kinkaid Clan is a really good example of how we can all work together—land and sea."

"They're pretty unique," Beth agreed. "At least, that's the impression I got from everything Moira said."

"Oh, there are other inclusive Clans out there. The Redstones come to mind. They've got more species under their banner than just about anybody else, but I don't think they have any water shifters. Although…come to think of it, they do have a very strong connection to water nowadays." Trevor scratched his jaw as if recalling something, and she was intrigued.

"Why is that?" Beth wanted to know. Maybe he was leading her down the garden path, trying deliberately to stir up her curiosity, but if so, he'd succeeded. Drat the man.

"Do you know what a water sprite is?" He answered her question with a question of his own.

"I've heard of them, but I've never run into one myself, if that's what you're asking." Why couldn't he just give her a straight answer?

"They're very powerful and very intensely

magical," he went on, as if he wasn't driving her crazy with suspense. "And one very notable family of them recently allied with the Redstone Clan via marriage. The second oldest brother, Steve, mated with Trisha Morrow, daughter of Admiral Morrow, who is very high up in the Spec Ops chain of command."

"Seriously?" Beth was surprised that any magical being could attain such power in a human-run military. Then again, the core group of bear shifters who had created Grizzly Cove were all said to be former military men.

"It's not that uncommon for magical folk who can pass for human to use their powers for good—or evil. The bad guys hide their true nature, of course. The good guys hide in plain sight for reasons of their own sometimes, too. But, after a very visible operation in Las Vegas a while back, the Morrows were well and truly outed to the magical community. Just about everyone who's interested knows their secret now."

"That's a shame," Beth said. Hiding was important to her. She'd hate to have everyone know her secrets.

"Trisha has three brothers. I've worked

with them all at one time or another when I was in the military. And I saluted the admiral more than a few times, as well," Trevor said with a friendly grin. "The bears have already requested their help with the leviathan, but word is, they're all out of contact, on critical military missions. When they get back in communication, I'm pretty sure they'll be on the way here if you all haven't solved the critter problem by then."

Trevor was looking out over the water, to the mouth of the cove, but she was watching him. She realized he really was a handsome man, once she got over being scared of his size.

"Why are you telling me all this? Isn't it privileged information or something?"

"Not really. So many of us know about it, it's hard to imagine our enemies don't have a clue what we're up to here. I would never betray any secrets, but this stuff is well known among the defenders of the cove— your people included. I figured it wouldn't hurt anything if you knew there was help— really good help—on the way, in case what you've got here so far can't handle it." Trevor looked at her, and she was struck by the chocolaty brown of his eyes. "I mean, they've done a great job so far. Urse's wards are top notch, from all accounts, and I expect her sister is brewing up something special to add to the protections, or maybe even extend them a bit. But the leviathan will have to be dealt with once and for all at some point in the near future. I'm not sure what that's going to take, but it could need a bit more firepower than they have here already."

"And you think the water sprites have the means necessary to defeat the creature?" Beth asked.

"I don't know," he answered with an air of honesty. "But they're pretty formidable. I'd be surprised if they can't do something." He was silent a moment before continuing. "Thing is, I'm pretty sure whatever the solution is, it's going to require all of us to work together."

Realization dawned. "Which is why you wanted me to make friends here, with Moira and the bears."

"That's part of it," he said. "But I also hoped that getting to know Moira would help ease some of your fears. Those of us who live on land all the time aren't really all that bad, Beth. I hope you're beginning to realize that." His voice had dropped to a low, intimate tone that sent a little frisson of…something…through her veins.

Was she attracted to this giant bear-man? Bright stars above. Maybe she was.

It didn't seem possible, but then again…

"And I admit, I have an ulterior motive to convincing you of that," he went on, and all her senses went on alert. Was the other shoe about to drop? Was he going to ruin what little trust he'd already earned?

"Ulterior motive, huh?" She hated the suspicion on her heart. He was going to let her down now. She just knew it. Might as well get it over with. "And what would that be, exactly?"

"Well…" He leaned from one foot to the other, drawing attention to his long jeans-clad legs. She couldn't help but notice how nicely he was put together, but she braced herself for whatever he was going to say next. "You know I was sent here to gather intel on the creatures out there watching the boundary of Urse's wards, right?"

She nodded, having learned that much at the dinner they'd shared with Grace and Jack.

"And I'm sending reports back to my

commanding officer that go up the line to Sam Kinkaid," he added. Again, she nodded. "Thing is…" He shifted his weight, seeming a bit uncomfortable. So far, his words hadn't been at all what she'd expected. "My first report was great, thanks to what you told me about your underwater vantage, but I've gotten a little sidetracked with carpentry work, and I'm concerned that I'll have nothing useful to report this week. I was wondering if you'd help me out."

She frowned. This wasn't what she'd expected him to say at all.

"How?" she asked, stymied by this whole direction of conversation.

"I was wondering if you'd swim with me, out near the mouth of the cove. Not too close to the border, of course, but I'd like to see what you see, and I'm pretty sure I'd need a guide to make sure I stay within the safe zone."

"Nansee doesn't want anyone swimming alone out there. We've been patrolling to make sure nobody gets too close," she told him.

"Which is exactly why I'd like you to be my escort," he agreed, smiling in a way that made her think that there might be some kind of loophole she was missing, but she couldn't see what.

"I suppose I could," she said, hesitating to agree fully, but seeing no valid reason to deny his request. "I'm scheduled for patrol tomorrow morning. If you can get some time away from the carpentry work, you could come along."

"I told the guys I was taking a day off tomorrow. I really do need to come up with something to report or I'm just wasting my time here. Reconnaissance is my real job, and the guys understand that." He gave her a rueful smile. "So, will you help me?"

Beth wasn't sure why her breath caught at the look in his eyes, but it took her a moment to regroup before she could answer. She nodded, stalling for time to formulate words.

"I'll swim with you tomorrow," she agreed, wondering if she'd just signed up for more than she could handle.

*

The next morning, Beth swam up under the boathouse and waited for Trevor to arrive. They'd agreed to meet in the lower level of the structure where shifters could make use of locker rooms for their belongings while they shifted and went into the water under cover of the building, coming out into the cove as clandestinely as possible.

It worked like a charm for water shifters, but Beth wasn't so sure how this was going to work for Trevor. Was he going to swim out with her in his human form? She hoped so. Although…he might be thinking he'd go in his grizzly form, which would be more problematic for her.

She had no doubt she could out-swim him in whatever form he chose. She could breathe underwater for one thing, which he could not. All she'd have to do was dive deep and swim fast, and she'd be away from him. Not that she was altogether certain she wanted to run from him. He was sort of growing on her. His calm, steady manner and deep voice had soothed her a little more each time they'd met.

He also intrigued her. He was just the sort of man she'd always been afraid of—big, muscular physique, trained to kill. She'd heard all about his badass arrival in town the first time he'd come to Grizzly Cove. He'd created quite a stir when he'd rappelled down a rope from a hovering black helicopter, right in front of the mayor's office.

She knew full well he could rip a man limb from limb if he chose to do so, but she had begun to think less about his physical strength and more about his gentle temperament. While she was sure he was lethal in many different ways, she was equally certain he would only use his ferocious skills when absolutely necessary.

Why she believed that so strongly, she wasn't sure, but she did. It made being around him easier.

"Hey, Beth." His voice came to her from just above the stairs that led down into the water.

She looked up to find him standing there, looking at her. She had maintained her mer form, the scales hiding the more intimate attributes of her body from view. Scales were as good as clothing when she was in her mer form, and she could selectively shift just parts of her body—her face or arms, for example, to reveal more human features, if she needed to.

"Hi, Trevor," she replied, watching his

reaction to her full mer features carefully.

She hadn't interacted with many non-mer in this form, but for some odd reason, she wanted Trevor to see her. And she wanted to be able to see his reaction to her full shift, which was what she was witnessing right now. If his expression was anything to go by, he looked fascinated…and pleased by what he saw. The thought sent a little tingle through her as she lazily used her fins to keep her steady in the water.

"Just give me a minute to stow my gear, and I'll be right with you," he said, sending her a gentle smile. "Will it bother you if I shift?"

"Right now?" she asked, feeling her throat go dry at the idea of him becoming his bear form in just a few minutes, within the confines of this structure. Suddenly, she felt claustrophobic.

"I thought I'd start out human and maybe shift when we get to the barrier. I can sense more in bear form, but I won't do it if it bothers you." His words and earnest tone helped the panic recede a bit.

"It's quite a distance to the mouth of the cove from here. Are you a strong swimmer?" She had to ask. Most humans couldn't handle that kind of long-distance swim, but she wasn't sure how a land-based shifter might compare.

"A big part of my military training involved swimming, diving and basically being wet and miserable for long periods of time with sand stuck in unmentionable places. This'll be a stroll in the park by comparison." He laughed, and she found herself smiling back at him. "Besides, I'm looking forward to stretching my muscles a bit. I haven't really had time for a good long swim in a while. It'll be fun."

Fun. Now, that was a novel concept. She'd never expected to hear a land shifter regard a long-distance swim as something *fun*. Apparently, she'd been wrong about quite a few things where land shifters were concerned.

Trevor waved and walked into the men's locker room, a short distance away. She waited for him, swimming little circles in the enclosed area under the boathouse. The water was nice and deep here, but she didn't dive. She didn't want Trevor to think she'd chickened out and left if he came out of the locker room to find her missing.

When he reappeared a few minutes later,

he was wearing a pair of green board shorts that made him look more like a buff surfer than a bear shifter. His muscles rippled as he moved, and he was stretching his arms as he walked back toward the stairs that led down into the water. Beth felt her mouth water as she got a good look at his arms and washboard abs. His legs were in perfect proportion to the rest of his long, lean, ripped form.

He was built on the massive side, but it was more from his tall stature than any extra bulkiness. He had the muscles of a hardworking giant, not a steroid pumped weightlifter. She devoured him with her eyes, powerless to stop her slack-jawed admiration of the hard planes of his body. Luckily, he seemed not to notice, and she was able to collect herself before he dipped his toes, cautiously at first, into the water.

The careful dip was followed by a leap and big splash as he cannon-balled into the water. She blinked in surprise as he surfaced a few feet away, grinning like a fool.

"Hope you don't mind. All at once is the best way to acclimate to the cool temperature. I'm good to go now, if you are. We go out underwater, right?"

She considered how they were going to affect a secret exit. There weren't really any loose humans in town yet, but the mer always practiced the utmost care when entering and leaving the water.

"How long can you hold your breath?" she asked him, wondering if he had the lung capacity of his bear when he was in human form.

"About five minutes," he replied quietly. "Is that enough?"

"Five minutes is double that of most well-trained humans," she replied, impressed. "It'll be more than enough. I'll lead, if you don't mind following me. We can surface a ways out so you can breathe."

"Sounds like a plan. Lead on, sweetheart."

The endearment sent a little jolt of pleasure through her body, but she did her best to ignore it. He probably called every female that. She shouldn't read anything into it.

CHAPTER FOUR

Trevor enjoyed the challenge of following Beth as she swam gracefully underwater, cutting through the current easily with her colorful tail. He hadn't really known what to expect, but her shimmering blue, green, and even hints of purple scales were beyond beautiful. She was breathtaking, here in her element.

He extended his arms, reaching to swim as fast as he could, but he knew she kept herself to a slow pace, just for him. There was absolutely no way he would ever be able to out-swim her, and until this point, he'd considered himself as good in the water as, if not better than, any Navy SEAL he'd ever met.

Trevor supposed it was good to understand one's limitations. Every once in a while, getting knocked out of your own complacency was useful. He understood now that he would never be able to compete with a mer in the water, which was good to know, both for himself and for his report. Even other shifters knew little about the secretive mer, so any intel—even something as simple as observations about their swimming capabilities—was valuable.

Of course, Kinkaid probably already knew more about the mer than Trevor would learn today. He'd had Moira feeding him information for a while now, and she herself was a water shifter. She was probably in a position to better judge other beings' abilities in a water environment than Trevor was, but he knew his CO would be pleased with the intel. There weren't any mermaids in Wyoming, but the men he worked with were sent all over the world and might need to know this information one day.

They'd never understand the sheer beauty of Beth's mer form, but that wasn't essential for his report. No, that was something

Trevor would hold dear to his heart, for now that he'd seen her, in all her scaled glory, he would never, ever forget it.

As he followed the sparkling colors of her tail fin through the chilly waters of the cove, he got a true appreciation for the way she moved in the water. He also found himself nearly bowled over by the beauty of her sleek body in motion. Her scales covered her feminine attributes like a swimsuit, but the outline of her svelte form was there, and he found it very attractive.

She was small, but fast, and he had to admit, he liked a woman who knew how to wear weapons. Strapped to her arms and torso were a number of sheathed blades in various sizes. He'd never thought much about fighting women before, but Beth had been part of what she'd called a hunting party. From what he'd been able to gather, hunting parties not only hunted for food to feed the pod, as their name implied, but also protected the pod from ocean threats.

She started heading upward, toward the surface, and he followed. He'd told her five minutes was his top limit for holding his breath, but the truth was, he could go a bit longer. He'd trained specifically to increase his lung capacity and had better control than most bears. Still, he was a bit rusty, so the break was welcome. He followed her to the surface, amazed as she shifted just her head and shoulders as they popped out of the water.

"You doing okay?" Beth asked as he surfaced next to her.

"Fine," he replied easily. "I just have to say, the partial shift is really impressive. How long can you hold it?"

She seemed surprised by his words. He looked away, to gauge where they'd come up. They were a good distance into the cove now, though he could see the shore was closer on one side than the other. It looked like she was making for one corner of the mouth of the cove, which made sense if they were going to swim across on a patrol pattern.

"Oh, we practice partial shifts from childhood. It's something we all do." Beth's eloquent shrug made it seem like no big deal, but among land shifters, partial shifts were difficult to hold and only for the strongest among them.

"I'm impressed," he told her. "Most of us have a partial shift battle form that's hard to keep hold of, but formidable if you can master it."

She tilted her head to one side, as if considering his words. "I'm not sure if it's the same for us. We practice shifting parts of our bodies, so that whatever might be visible out of the water looks human, while we retain the ability to breathe and swim like mer. It's useful when encountering humans on the open water, though we try to avoid them, if at all possible."

He found her explanation fascinating. Actually, he found everything about her fascinating…and very, very attractive.

"I have to dive to retrieve my trident before we get to the barrier. If you want to wait here a minute, I'll get it. It's just below us here. Then, we can go on."

He nodded, and she disappeared from view with a flash of her bright scales just below the surface. Trevor sank down into the water to see if he could follow her progress, but she was already gone. She was *fast*.

Beth was glad to get away from Trevor for a minute. She'd found it a bit nerve-wracking to have him watching her so closely as they swam. She could actually feel his eyes studying her, and she wasn't sure what to make of the emotions that brought up within her.

She felt a giddy sort of girlish excitement that she didn't recall ever feeling before herself, but thought she recognized from observing some of the younger members of the pod. Then again, her youth had been anything but normal, so the fact that she hadn't experienced something didn't mean much. She was old enough to recognize the nervousness that young girls seemed to feel when they were around an attractive boy.

Beth was floored to realize she was feeling that now. Her rise to adulthood hadn't included such normal things as dating and being around boys her own age. Until she'd come to the pod, she hadn't been around any other mer—or even any other people—except those her stepfather allowed in his domain. And those were folks she'd rather not be around at all.

She retrieved her trident from where she'd hidden it, secured by a sturdy number of kelp vines. This was her special hiding spot that she'd scoped out and claimed when she'd first come to the cove. Each mer had their own unique space in the cove. Their own territory, if you will. This kelp bed was hers. At night, she would sleep here, among the caressing vines and dream of a life free from worry, and a home of her own where nothing and no one could ever hurt her again.

Dreams. That's all they were. She was enough of a realist to understand that life was hard and fantasies of security and love never came true. If she'd been above the waterline, she would have sighed. As it was, she retrieved her trident and headed for the surface, girding herself mentally to deal with the inquisitive bear shifter waiting up there for her.

As she rose, she noted that he, too, was submerged, seeming to look for her in the dim waters of the cove. Was he that nosy? Probably. He was an intelligence expert, after all. Discovering things was his stock in trade. But she'd thought he would be enjoying his surface time, knowing he would be called upon to hold his breath again as they swam for the cove entrance.

He was a funny bear. He didn't do anything she expected of him.

She held her trident as she'd been taught.

Neither leading with it nor letting it trail behind. It stayed at her side, ready for use and away from anyone or anything that might try to take it from her. She met Trevor's gaze as she pulled alongside him, just below the surface of the water. He seemed to be admiring her trident...and her body, as well.

If she could have blushed in full mer form, her cheeks would be flaming. As it was, the blue tint of her scales went a bit purple at the edges, but she had hope that the bear shifter wasn't familiar enough with her kind to know that was a sign of mer embarrassment.

She pointed toward the surface, and he nodded. Once again, she did the partial shift of just her head and shoulders as she emerged above the waterline. She kept her trident below, to avoid any casual observation.

"That's quite the weapon," Trevor said, having broken the surface only feet away from her.

"Thanks. Most of the hunters have them," she said, then wanted him to understand a bit more of what her trident meant to her. "It's probably my favorite possession. We don't need much in the sea, but I really like my knives and especially my trident. When I lived ashore as a girl, I wasn't allowed to even touch anything that might resemble a weapon. Having the freedom to not only touch, but own and use these tools of my position means a lot to me."

Maybe she'd said too much. He seemed to be assessing her for a moment before he replied.

"I understand. Although I have been known to carry firearms and even explosives, I've always enjoyed bladed weapons more than just about any of the other tools in my arsenal. There's something so elegant about them. Like that little titanium number you've got strapped to your left arm. I usually carry a knife from that same company in my boot. I recognize the logo. They make a nice array of blades for just about every occasion." He nodded toward her left shoulder, with the knife strapped to it below the waterline.

He had to be pretty observant to recognize the small logo on the handle, she realized. And he probably knew more about weapons than she did, but she had been learning quickly since she'd joined the pod and had very astute teachers.

"That one was a gift from Sirena, my old hunting party leader. It was one of hers. She taught me how to use it underwater, and when the lessons were over, she gave it to me to keep. I got the larger one on my right arm shortly after that, once I'd earned a bit of credit for helping one of the pod families. They gave it to me as payment."

"I was wondering how you managed to buy things when you spend most of your time underwater," Trevor said with a smile as they stroked lazily toward their ultimate destination. They would have to do more serious swimming shortly, but for now, she was enjoying talking with him here, in her element, where she felt safest.

"We barter a lot. Things get passed around from those who either don't need them anymore or don't want them, to those who do, but we don't really need much when we're in the ocean. The sea provides us with almost everything we need." She thought about the trident in her hand. "Although we do have contacts on shore that procure or make special things for us, like my trident."

"That's not something you can buy out of a catalog, I'll wager," Trevor replied.

"You're right," she agreed. "They're specially made for us, sized for each owner by the smith who makes them, and imbued with protective magic at the moment of their creation. Or so the story goes."

"Magic?" Trevor asked. "Are they made by a mer or by a mage?"

"I think he's a mage. Or maybe a series of mages all around the world who've gone into business with mer pods. All I know is our guy lives on a little island somewhere near Seattle. When I was finally made a member of the hunting party, Sirena and the girls took me ashore one night on his island, and we knocked on his door. He kept bathrobes in a beach cabana for us, so I think he was used to having mer guests. They measured my height and my arm reach, and then, he looked at me for a few minutes and asked a few questions about my personal tastes in style. He also asked about my fin coloration, I think. We spent about a half hour talking, and then, he told us to come back in a week with payment."

"What did he want for payment?" Trevor asked quietly, his brows drawing together in a frown.

"Not what I expected," Beth admitted.

BIANCA D'ARC

"No money changed hands. Instead, he asked for some rarities from the ocean floor. Nothing irreplaceable or endangered, but all things land dwellers would have a hard time procuring. The girls and I thought of it as a scavenger hunt. Over the next week, we had a lot of fun gathering the things on his list. He'd given us a plastic card on a chain that Sirena wore around her neck. On it were printed a number of different items he wanted us to look for. A certain kind of sea urchin spine. Particular shells with intricate patterns. Fish and plants that only live at very deep depths. Even a specific kind of rare crab. That sort of thing. He let us judge which items and how many. I thought we skimped a bit, but when we went back the following week, he seemed very pleased with the things we gave him, and he, in turn, gave me the trident."

"It suits you. From what I saw, the curves are elegant and appear to be quite effective for their purpose," Trevor commented as they stroked along on the surface. They weren't getting anywhere fast, but she was enjoying the conversation too much for it to end too soon. "I assume you've trained with it in the water, but what about on land?"

"The trident is a water weapon," Beth admitted. "All my training has been in the sea."

Trevor frowned some more. "Don't take this the wrong way, but I could teach you a bit of self-defense on land, if you want. It's not good for a woman not to know at least some basics in the world we live in right now."

He was offering to teach her how to protect herself? She was taken aback by the offer, but she knew she needed more skills if she was ever going to feel safe out of the water. Learning how to hunt and fight underwater had done a lot for her self-esteem, but on land, she was still as scared as a fish on the hook.

But to be trained by him? A scary bear shifter? Beth wasn't sure she had the courage to even attempt something like that.

"It's kind of you to offer..." she began, suddenly not wanting to talk anymore. "But I'll have to think about it." She rushed her words, eager to be done with this conversation—something she wouldn't have imagined even a few moments ago. "Shall we swim some more? I really should be on patrol by now. The others are probably waiting for me."

Trevor knew when to back down. He'd spooked her, and he had only himself to blame for ruining the easy camaraderie they'd shared up to that point. Oh, well. Maybe there would be other chances. He just had to be patient and work on gentling her again—getting her used to him and confident in the idea that he wasn't going to try to hurt her.

"Sure. Let's swim," he answered her query with false cheer. "Five minute breaks for me to breathe?" he asked, just for something to say.

"Sounds good," she answered in a clipped tone before she submerged without saying anything more.

Okay, then. Looked like it was time to swim. Trevor took a deep breath and struck out below the surface, following the flash of his mermaid's tail.

They took the swim in stages, pausing only to let him breathe quickly between the long underwater stretches. They were employing a bit of stealth by swimming underwater and coming up rarely, but Trevor saw it more as a training mission because there weren't any non-magical visitors in town just now, and he really needed the exercise.

Sitting around in town wasn't the hard physical training he was used to. The carpentry helped, but he was used to doing more than just lifting lumber into place and using pneumatic tools. The swim was good for him. It tested one of the skills he hadn't had much call to use lately.

When they got closer to the southern point of the cove's mouth, Beth slowed and surfaced. She spoke briefly with another mermaid she introduced to Trevor as Janice before the other woman swam off into the cove. Trevor understood that Janice had been waiting for Beth to take over her position on patrol. Shift change, as it were.

Janice was friendly enough and even winked at Trevor as she swam off. She seemed amused to see him with Beth, as if their pairing was some sort of cosmic joke. Trevor wasn't deterred by the orange-finned mermaid's attitude. He liked Beth, despite her rough edges, and he'd find a way to make her understand that he wasn't the enemy and that he would die before he hurt her—or give his life to protect her.

Whoa. His thoughts had turned more serious than he'd realized, but something about Beth compelled him and raised every protective instinct he possessed. He didn't really understand it, but the prickly mermaid stirred feelings he hadn't experienced in a very long time—if ever.

Speaking of strange feelings... As they took the patrol position closer to the ward than he'd ever been, Trevor started to feel a tingling of magic. He wasn't as sensitive to magic in his human form. He'd have to go bear if he wanted to get the best possible sense of what he was seeing and feeling out here. He just hoped it didn't freak Beth out too much.

Then again, it might help in getting her used to his other form. She'd need to be comfortable around him no matter which shape he wore if they were going to be friends...or more.

He stopped himself again. Where were these strange thoughts coming from? He couldn't expect much of any relationship he might form with Beth. It was pretty clear she'd been hurt badly in her past, and she had a lot of baggage from whatever it was that had made her so skittish. Trevor honestly didn't know if he would ever be able to help her overcome her fears, but he would try.

Trying to help her in that way was a far cry from having a romantic relationship with her, but somehow, that's where his mind went lately, whenever he thought of her. Sex with her would be like nothing he'd ever had before. He was sure of it. But why he was so sure, only the Goddess knew.

"Do you mind if I shift?" Trevor asked her, trying to get his mind off sex and back onto his mission. Thinking about making love to Beth right now could only get him into trouble.

Her eyes went wide, and he suspected she was close to panic mode, but she nodded. He was impressed. She must realize she could easily swim away if he somehow went berserk and threatened her. Plus, she was heavily armed with all sorts of blades, including that wicked looking trident.

He had to admit, he was a bit envious. That trident looked like something he'd love to learn how to use efficiently. But he was a blade nut from way back. Swords, knives, even spears were things of beauty to him.

She put a bit of space between them. She

tried to seem casual about it, but he noticed her backing off. He let her go, not wanting to scare her any more than he had to.

"Really?" she asked, surprising him. He'd expected either a yes or no, not a query. She didn't look too thrilled by his desire to go furry, but he really had no choice. He thought he'd already explained why, but maybe she needed more rationalization. He tried to be patient with her fears.

"I think I mentioned that I sense things in my fur that I don't always pick up on in my skin," he told her. "And my bear form loves the water. And fish. I especially enjoy stalking salmon when they're running. My bear side really likes fresh sushi," he added with a smile.

His words made her smile faintly, and she backed off another foot, looking resigned. "Well, okay then. I'll wait for you over here, but I hope you'll understand if I don't swim too close to you when you're…uh…furry."

"No worries. I won't be able to speak, but feel free to talk to me if you think I need to know anything. I'll come up for air occasionally, and you can fill me in if there's anything to say."

She agreed and backed away a little more.

He tried not to take it personally. She was really afraid of his bear form, for some reason, but he couldn't help what had to happen now. He had to shift to perform his job to the best of his abilities. Hopefully, she'd learn that he was the same person in his skin as he was in his fur. Maybe his senses were sharper and his instincts a bit more wild, but he wouldn't do anything as a bear that he wouldn't do as a human. Maybe she'd figure that out as they swam.

Trevor submerged, shucked his swim shorts and arranged them into a solid line of fabric that the bear form could grab in its teeth. No sense losing a good pair of shorts. He'd worn them to spare Beth's sensibilities, and if he shifted back to human for the swim home, he'd probably want to put them on again.

He shifted fast, grabbing his shorts with his teeth before they had any chance to sink. He noticed that Beth had kept an eye on him throughout. She'd backed away even more, but he was okay with that. He'd give her as much space as she needed to get used to him. When he rose above the water with his shorts hanging out of his mouth, she smiled at him in surprise and might have even giggled a bit.

CHAPTER FIVE

She didn't say anything as they set off along the boundary. He could feel it pulsing with pure magic now, tingling against his fur. They stayed a safe distance from the edge of the barrier, swimming along and looking for potential problems. Beth led the way with her trident, and Trevor got to admire the way she moved, the weapon kept close by her side. He had no doubt she knew how to handle the spear with three blades on one end that had been custom made for her. Her skill spoke for itself with every move she made.

Trevor chastised himself for watching her

when he should be making observations about the magical ward that kept the cove safe. He set to work, trying to take mental notes on everything he saw so he could report back to his superiors. This might be the only chance he got to swim this close to the ward, so he had to make the most of the opportunity.

Trevor kept his bear form all the way across the mouth of the cove. The ward bowed in a bit at the widest point and Beth was good about keeping them a standard distance from the edge of the ward. He noticed the smaller multi-tentacled creatures swimming parallel to their path on the other side, in the open ocean, and he did his best to take note of their dimensions and attributes.

Nobody had made detailed drawings yet of the creatures, and reports varied widely. One of the tasks Trevor had been assigned was to get more specific details about the leviathan and its army of smaller minions, if at all possible.

He wished he'd brought an underwater camera with him, but he hadn't realized they'd be able to get close enough to really see the creatures. He might have to mount a second expedition in his human form so he could use whatever technology he could have flown in on short notice to make more accurate records of these creatures.

As it was, he was going to spend a few hours with pencils and paper, doing his best to draw what he'd just seen. He'd ask for Beth's opinion before he sent his artwork off to his superiors. She and her fellow patrollers had probably seen more than they ever wanted of the creatures.

But even more than their physical characteristics, in his bear form, he was able to better assess their magical attributes. Trevor had trained to note subtle differences in magical energies, and he was concentrating hard on each of the malevolent creatures that watched them from just beyond the barrier of Urse's magical ward.

He swam slowly as they neared the other side of the cove mouth, studying hard. He would do his best to return with high-tech equipment to get still and video images of the creatures, if at all possible, but the information he was gathering right now was critical. He was the man the Wraiths depended on to assess the magical threats they sometimes faced in the field. This was his true specialty, though he had many other equally important skills.

Trevor took his time, knowing what he reported would be taken with the utmost seriousness. He wanted it to be as complete and accurate as possible because lives could very well depend on what he said.

By the time he was satisfied with his own observations, he could tell Beth was getting impatient. He swam a bit faster in his human form, so he surfaced and shifted. She surprised him by asking if he wanted to take a short break on the beach before they headed back.

"There's a good spot on the rocks where we can observe without being seen from the ocean," she told him. "And sometimes, the creatures rise out of the water to look, or wave a threatening tentacle in our direction."

Trevor was intrigued by the idea and wanted to witness the phenomenon himself, if he could. Plus, a break from the water would be good before they started back. His skin was getting pruney.

Sure, they probably could've arranged to take a vehicle of some kind to the mouth of the cove and just do the swim across, but

Trevor had wanted to spend as much time with Beth as possible, to hopefully acclimate her to his animal side. He thought maybe the plan had worked, since she seemed less afraid of him than when he'd first broached the subject of going bear.

He had his shorts looped over one arm as they set out for shore. She'd just have to deal with the few moments when he'd be stark naked while he pulled the shorts back on. If she was going to live in Grizzly Cove for any length of time, she was going to have to get used to seeing shifters running around naked from time to time. Of course, she could always look away.

Some perverse part of his nature hoped she wouldn't. He wanted to know if she was attracted to him, even though he thought the possibility was remote. If she looked, well, then, the chances were good that maybe— just maybe—she might be the tiniest bit interested.

She motioned for him to precede her out of the water, and he didn't hesitate to stride up the beach, giving her a good view of his butt. He pulled on his shorts casually, not wanting to embarrass her if he caught her looking. Plus, he could hear the rustle of fabric behind him. Those modest mermaids had stashed a towel or something behind a rock.

He should have realized. Not one of those ladies seemed the type to lounge around naked where somebody might see them. They were even more cautious about their dual nature being discovered than land-based shifters were.

When the sound of fabric rustling died down behind him, he finally turned. He was just buttoning the top button on his shorts. He looked up…and she was looking at him. Not just looking. *Staring*. Almost leering, actually. In the nicest possible way. His ego inflated just a bit.

He'd be damned. She might just be a little attracted to him if the way she was staring at his bod was any indication. Well, hallelujah. He hadn't completely lost his touch with the fair sex.

Though to be fair, it wasn't just a dalliance he had in mind when he thought about Beth. There was something about her…

No time to daydream now. If he wasn't mistaken, one of the creatures was checking them out from beyond the barrier.

Trevor set to work, observing and taking mental note of the creature's behavior. He asked Beth some pertinent questions, and they spent a good half hour watching the various displays he supposed were meant to be threatening. He found it fascinating, though he realized somewhat belatedly that Beth seemed to jump at the especially energetic movements of the enemy.

Trevor put his arm around her shoulders after she yelped involuntarily when one of the larger minions slapped its tentacles down on the water only about twenty yards away from them. It was clearly angry. Or taunting. Maybe frustrated. It was hard to tell. Trevor would have to come back and study these creatures some more if he wanted to be able to interpret their movements more reliably.

"Can we go now?" Beth asked in a small voice, accepting his touch and almost clinging to his side.

"I'm sorry, sweetie. Of course we can. Don't worry. Ol' ugly out there can't get to us. That barrier is good and strong and unlike just about anything I've ever encountered before. It'll hold." He tried to reassure her, rubbing her arm in what he hoped was a soothing way. "Do you have to go back across? How long does your patrol duty last?"

"I made special arrangements to take you around this morning. There's plenty of coverage. I can go back anytime," she admitted. Trevor took that as another sign that she just might be interested in him. She'd thought ahead and set this up so they could spend time together. Nice.

"All right, then. Let's go. By the way, lunch is on me if you care to join me. I was hoping to eat at the bakery after our swim." Couldn't hurt to ask, he figured. He really wanted her to say yes, but wasn't sure she would spend more time with him today.

She moved away, out from under his arm, and seemed to consider his words. "Yes, okay," she finally agreed in a breathy voice. "Thanks."

The swim back was uneventful. Trevor stayed in his human form, and Beth felt safe enough with him now that she swam by his side. He had a much greater lung capacity than she'd expected and was very good in the water. If he had gills, he would fit right in with her pod, but that need to surface every now and then made her feel more like she was swimming with some of her playful dolphin friends, instead of a badass bear shifter.

The conversation over lunch was general and light—enjoyable in the extreme, actually. It was only after they'd finished eating and were lingering over coffee and dessert that things turned serious again with the arrival of Urse at the bakery. She came over to their table to say hello, and Trevor immediately started talking about his rather astute observations of the ward.

"I haven't been out in the water to look at it the way you and my husband have," Urse said. "But it's really intriguing to hear the way my magic is manifesting below the surface. I've never really done a ward over a body of water before, so I didn't know what to expect, but it seems to be working adequately enough. At least, John thinks so," she added modestly.

"It's more than just adequate, ma'am," Trevor said respectfully. "It's far superior to anything I've ever encountered before, and I've seen wards like yours a time or two around the globe. Ancient wards, mostly, that were put up by mages long gone. I think your wards will stand the tests of time like those. It's rather humbling to see them so fresh and new, and powerful."

Beth was floored to see Urse—mate of the Alpha bear, mighty *strega* in her own right—actually blush at Trevor's praise.

"I'd like to discuss some of my notes with you before I file my report, if you're willing," Trevor went on.

"Well, I'm just here to pick up our lunch order, and then, I'm going to eat with my husband in his office while we talk over some plans for additional construction with Nansee. You're welcome to come by after that. Maybe in an hour? I'm sure John would like to hear what you've discovered today."

"And if Nansee's free, would you ask her to stick around for a bit?" Trevor asked, nodding in agreement with Urse's plan. "I want to be certain the information I pass along to my CO and, ultimately, Kinkaid is as accurate as possible. And, of course, I'm happy to share all my findings with you and your people. I'm authorized to give all aid and full disclosure on this job, which makes my task a whole lot easier."

They agreed on the time, and then, Urse left with a friendly round of goodbyes to everyone in the bakery. She was very popular, Beth saw, which boded well for the Alpha couple. If a leader was popular, the whole community usually thrived, as was the case with her adopted pod. Nansee was by far the favorite to lead the pod, and she did a great job of it, making decisions for all based on what was best for the community as a whole, not just her as an individual. That's why their pod prospered while others—it was rumored—didn't do quite as well.

Not that the really large pods saw much of one another. It was a really big ocean, after all, and there weren't all that many mer in it. There was another pod down south, off the coast of Central America, but Beth's pod claimed the territory from the Bering Sea up near Alaska, all the way down the Pacific coast of the United States and westward to about the middle of the Pacific Ocean, though they kept relatively close to land most of the year.

"I really want to thank you for taking me around this morning, Beth," Trevor said as she refocused her attention on her coffee.

It was a mark of how comfortable she'd become with him that she'd allowed her attention to drift while in his presence. She didn't feel the need to be perpetually on guard with him anymore. Not after meeting his bear side and swimming with him—in both forms—in the cove. Something important had changed this morning, and she wasn't sure how far reaching the implications might yet go.

"I was happy to do it," she replied politely. "You swim really well." It was only the truth, even if it was also a compliment.

"I train hard in many different environments, but I've always loved swimming. I've had a lot of opportunities to use that skill both in military training and in the field, but today was exceptional in many ways. You're amazing in the water, Beth. There's no way I could keep up with you if you didn't want me to. Thanks for making allowances and slowing your pace. Swimming with you today is an experience I will never forget."

She was humbled by the true admiration she thought she heard in his voice.

"I'd like to ask one more favor of you, if I may," he went on, sparing her the need to reply. "I'm going to draw up some of my impressions of the creatures we saw today. I'd like to run the art by you, just to make sure I've got it right, before I send my report. Will you have a few minutes later tonight? Maybe we could meet for dinner or after, if you have a few minutes to spare?"

Was he asking her out? Could she really spend a second meal with him in a single day?

Beth chastised herself inwardly. She shouldn't get so excited. It was only work for him, after all. He wasn't interested in her romantically. And even if he was—she couldn't deal with that sort of complication. Not now. Maybe not ever. Not with all the baggage she carried from her early life. Simply put, she was scared of getting involved with any man, but particularly wary of a strong Alpha-type like Trevor. He was too…overpowering.

Too attractive, too. Too easy to fall in love with and be left either broken-hearted or crushed under his thumb. She frowned at the dark thought.

"Not dinner," she blurted out before she realized how rude she sounded. She tried to soften her response. "Maybe we could meet back here for dessert around seven or eight? I can look at the drawings then, but I can only spare about a half hour." She didn't want him to think she was setting up some sort of rendezvous. She had to keep things strictly business between them.

Didn't she?

Trevor figured he'd pushed Beth about as far as he could for one day. She'd seemed so at ease with him until just a few minutes ago. He'd said something wrong. Pushed too hard. Whatever it was, he thought a strategic retreat was in order for now. Plus, he had to do some sketches of those sea monsters. He'd start now and hopefully have something to show Nansee and the Alpha couple when he went to meet with them in an hour.

He'd get their input and then have something more polished to show Beth tonight. His preliminary report to his CO was due this evening, so he'd finalize things and send them off before he hit the hay tonight. That ought to keep his boss happy for a while.

Trevor took his leave of Beth and headed for his hotel room. He had to clean up and drag out the drawing supplies he always brought with him when he was on recon missions like this. He'd have just enough time to get a few sketches started before he'd have to leave again for his meeting at town hall. His so-called day off work was certainly filling up fast.

He arrived only a few minutes late. He'd started sketching, and before he knew it, he'd had to run to keep his appointment. Luckily, the distances along Main Street in Grizzly Cove weren't far. The town just wasn't that big yet, though there were signs of construction everywhere, and he had a feeling the town might just continue to grow, given its success so far.

Of course, their success had also drawn unwanted attention from the leviathan, but with any luck, they'd be able to sort out a permanent solution to that problem in short order. And they'd be doing the entire world a favor if they sent that evil thing and its friends back from whence they had come.

CHAPTER SIX

Trevor's meeting with the Alpha couple and the pod leader went well. They'd all been very interested in his observations of the magical ward and his preliminary sketches of some of the creatures he'd seen. Nansee, in particular, had helped him identify four distinct types of creature that had only slight, but notable, differences. Trevor took notes to clarify his sketches before he showed them to Beth.

Nansee had also been very helpful when Trevor mentioned wanting to go out to the barrier again with some kind of underwater photography gear. She said she knew a someone who could be there by the next morning with all the gear he'd want for both still photos and hi-res video. She made a few phone calls, and suddenly, Trevor's morning was booked. Which was a good thing. Especially when Nansee insisted he take Beth along with him again.

Trevor wasn't altogether certain why Nansee insisted on sending Beth with him. Maybe Beth was her informant. Or maybe the pod leader had noticed something between him and Beth and wanted to encourage it. He wasn't sure what her motivations were, but he was thankful for any opportunity to be near the pretty young mermaid. Something about her called out to him.

He wanted to protect her. He wanted to make her laugh. Above all, he wanted to make her feel safe and lose the fear that seemed to be her near-constant companion.

Trevor left the meeting in town hall with a spring in his step. He went back to his hotel room to work on refining his drawings, in preparation for showing them to Beth later that evening. He also spent a little time typing up his report on the laptop he was using while on this mission. Normally, he wouldn't use any sort of gear that could be stolen or infiltrated, but his CO had weighed the risks and dropped some of the usual precautions on this mission. For one thing, Grizzly Cove itself provided ample security against enemy infiltration. In fact, if somebody with ill intent somehow managed to get into the town, Trevor wished him good luck getting back out.

Being in this town was almost as safe as being back at the Wraiths' HQ on a Wyoming mountaintop. Strangers were easily spotted, and there were so many folks in town who were sensitive to magic—between all the bears, the mer, the *strega* sisters, the shaman and the visiting priestess—that evil wouldn't stand a chance of moving in with nobody noticing.

Then, there was the ward. That permanent magical barrier that protected the cove also stretched over the main part of town, as well. Nothing evil could cross that barrier—either by land or sea. Grizzly Cove was probably more secure at this point than just about any other place on Earth, even if it was besieged by the leviathan from the ocean.

Trevor made it a point to get to the

bakery a bit early that night, opting to get dinner there and just stay and wait for Beth to arrive for dessert. He'd put his afternoon to good use and had come up with some sketches he was ready to send along to his CO as soon as Beth critiqued them. If he'd missed something or didn't catch some detail correctly, she would know, and he would have a chance to fix it before he took digital images of his art, encrypted it and sent it.

He just hoped Beth wasn't skittish with him. If she was, he'd try his best not to let it get him down. It seemed like he took two steps forward, one step back with this girl all the time, but as long as they were making progress, he was okay with it. He'd give her all the time she needed. Well...until he had to leave town. He hoped they'd be able to get beyond her fears by then. If they couldn't, he supposed he would think about Beth for the rest of his life. The one that got away. An appropriately fishy thought for a mermaid.

He was chuckling inwardly when she opened the door to the bakery, setting off the little tinkling bell just above the glass door. It was easy to smile when he saw her, which was an odd feeling for him. Trevor wasn't known in Spec Ops circles as a man who smiled often—or at all, actually. He was usually expected to growl and cuss rather than smile and moderate his tone and his words. Then again, he was seldom around women in his line of work.

Despite the fact that most of his colleagues probably thought he'd crawled out from under a rock fully grown, his mother had raised him to be a gentleman when dealing with females. Somehow, those old lessons had come easily to the forefront when he'd met Beth. There was something so strong, yet fragile, about her. She was a contradiction—swimming expertly with that sharp trident of hers, yet cringing from a harsh tone of voice. He wanted to know what made her tick. What made her shy away. And what finally caused her to stand up for herself.

He wanted the be the one who finally helped her regain her footing in what must be a world gone mad with the leviathan chasing her from the one place she'd seemed to feel safe. He wanted her to feel secure in all places, at all times. She deserved that, and he wanted to be the one to give that to her.

"I see you already ordered dessert," Beth

said, coming over to his table and eyeing the array of pastries he had on a plate at the center of the table while he sorted through his papers in preparation for their meeting. "Or are those all for you?" She sat with a small smile that made him feel ten feet tall. Maybe they weren't going backward, after all.

"I asked Tina for a selection, and she came up with this. If you'd rather have something else, just let me know, and I'll get it for you. Would you like coffee or tea? Or something else to drink?" He was halfway standing when she waved him back down.

"I'll start with this honey bun," she said, taking the confection and its associated sheet of waxed paper and positioning it in front of her. "And we'll go from there. I might want something to drink later, but I'll get it. Thanks for setting up the platter of goodies. That was very thoughtful."

"No problem." He retook his seat and neatened his papers. Now that the time had come, he found he was a little nervous about showing her his artwork. In this town that portrayed itself as an artists' colony, his sketches seemed somehow on trial.

Even though Trevor knew the whole artists' colony thing was just a cover and the guys who were producing sculptures and paintings weren't really serious about it, he felt a bit of pressure to prove that he had some small amount of talent. It was odd, really. Trevor had always enjoyed drawing. Doodling sketches of the scenes around him had always been a pleasant pastime for him on his various missions around the world.

In fact, he had a whole suitcase full of sketches of different people and landmarks he'd seen in his travels. Being a soldier, and now, a soldier of fortune, meant he spent a lot of time on the road. It wasn't all action. Sure, there were firefights on occasion, and concentrated moments of absolute mayhem, but most of the time, it was just sitting around, waiting for the action to start. Pre-positioning. Getting the lay of the land. And in his case, working covertly to assess the intel.

Mostly that involved sitting around observing. And how better to observe than with a sketchpad in hand, pretending to be a tourist? Cameras were seen as a threat in many parts of the world, but a guy with a pencil and a tablet of paper was viewed more as an eccentric than any real danger. He'd used that ploy many times to his advantage, and had the sketches to prove it.

He'd drawn everything from the Eiffel Tower to the pyramids, from one end of the world to the other. Looking through that suitcase was like looking through the past, at the entirety of his career and travels. Someday, he promised himself, he'd frame a few of the better pieces and put them up in his home. If he ever made himself a permanent den.

A lot depended on whether or not he ever found a mate to share his life. Of course, if she didn't like his art, he would keep it all in the suitcase. No matter how much he'd like to display it, the mate's desires always came first. He knew that from having watched his parents. They were as in love today as they had been from the moment they'd met, and Trevor wanted that for himself. Someday. If the Goddess was kind.

"Are those papers what you wanted me to look at?" Beth asked after finishing a bite of her honey bun. Trevor had been so consumed with his own thoughts, he hadn't really realized she'd been watching him the whole time.

"Yes." He fumbled a bit with the stack of

drawings. He'd done four in the time allotted, of the four major kinds of creatures he'd seen that morning. He handed over the stack as she wiped her hands on a napkin then held the papers by their edges, so as not to smudge his pencil work.

"Oh, these are good," she said, at first sight. Her expression went still as she really looked at what he'd drawn. "You've got a gift," she mused as she flipped through the sketches, studying each in detail. "I call this one the streamer because of all the long tendrils that follow after it as it swims." She pointed to the tentacle details he'd painstakingly drawn from memory. "And I call this one the clamshell because of the shape of its torso. See the way it bulges here. You've captured it perfectly. This one, I call the sponge because of the irregular pockmarks on its skin." She flipped to another page. "Finally, I named this one El Diablo because it was one of these that almost killed me when my hunting party was being chased by them all on the way here." She shuddered and handed the papers back, averting her gaze as if she didn't want to see the creatures anymore.

"You fought one of these?" Trevor kept

El Diablo's portrait on top, turning it to face him, so he could study the creature.

"Not really fought. More like ran away after trying to fend it off with my trident. If Jetty's mate hadn't come when he did, we'd all be dead." She looked away and took a mechanical bite of her honey bun, all enjoyment gone from her face as she recalled the close brush she'd had with evil.

"I heard he used some of his personal shield magic to get you all back to the cove," Trevor said, hoping she might open up to him if he gave her the opportunity.

"He did more than that. He actually fought the leviathan from the deck of his little boat. I've never seen anything braver...or more foolhardy. It's a miracle we all survived, though Sirena was badly injured, of course."

"She's mated to the doctor now, right?" Trevor asked, though he already knew the answer. He was just trying to make conversation and keep Beth—touchy as she was—on a friendly footing. Also, reminding her that her friends had found happiness among the bears of Grizzly Cove wasn't necessarily a bad thing.

"Yes, hard as it is to believe," Beth

admitted. "I wasn't happy about it at first, but he's a good swimmer."

That must be high praise coming from a mer, Trevor reasoned. "Polar bear shifter, isn't he?" Again, he already knew the answer. Sven and he went all the way back to their time in the Special Forces. They weren't best friends or anything, but they'd worked together a few times.

Beth nodded. "They're better in the water than other bears, I gather. Of course, you did pretty well this morning. If I didn't say so before, I was impressed with your bear's ability to navigate the currents."

"Thank you." Now, why did he feel like he'd just been crowned king of all he surveyed? This small mer woman had the ability to affect his state of mind like no being he'd ever encountered. A word of praise from her, and suddenly, he felt happiness bloom in his chest. It wasn't cool. Not for a warrior who prided himself on his badass rep.

No, this wouldn't do at all. He had to get better control of himself and his emotions around her. He wanted her to feel happy and safe, but his own feelings had to be kept under wraps.

"Nansee tells me we're going out tomorrow afternoon with some high-tech gear to try to capture images of the creatures beyond the ward," she said, changing the subject.

"Yeah. I hope you don't mind that she volunteered you for the job."

"Mind? No, not at all," she said softly. "I'm not crazy about getting too close to the ward, you understand, but as long as we stay at the distance we were at today, it's all good."

"I don't plan to take any chances," Trevor assured her.

The bell above the door tinkled as the last of the patrons left. It was only them and Tina left in the bakery. Trevor supposed her mate would be along to see her home safely—not that there was any crime in Grizzly Cove, at the moment, but mates tended to want to look after one another, from what he'd observed of his own parents' bond.

That meant Trevor and Beth should probably be leaving, as well, so Tina could close up and go home to spend time with her mate. Loath as he was to end the evening, Trevor began stacking the few plates they'd used, to help Tina clear the mess faster, as was only polite. The pastries had all been finished a while ago, and he and Beth were down to their last sips of coffee.

"I guess she'll want to lock up soon," Beth said as she watched him organizing the used dishes.

Was it his imagination, or did she sound sort of…forlorn at the prospect of leaving? Trevor tried to hide his pleased reaction.

"Can I walk you home?" he asked, then a thought occurred to him. "Where are you staying?"

Beth lowered her eyes. "Like most of the pod, I'm sleeping in the cove for now. That's why there's such a building boom going on. We want places to rest on land, as well as in the water, since we're coming out of the cove regularly now to dine on shore and go shopping. The sea lifestyle isn't practical when you start accumulating objects like clothing and art that can't remain submerged. Now that we're here, we need land dwellings. The lockers at the boathouse are sufficient for now, but they'll quickly fill up as we begin to acquire things." She stood, and he followed suit, taking the used dishes back to the counter for Tina.

"You're actually being of great service to us, working on the construction projects around town," Beth went on. "I'm hoping to get a room at the boarding house that's nearing completion, or maybe even spring for one of the hotel rooms you're finishing, if I find I don't want to wait that long. It'll depend on how much it costs, though."

She lowered her eyes again at the mention of money, and Trevor frowned. The hotel wasn't that expensive. The owner set a special rate for shifters.

"Are you short of funds?" he asked in a low voice, not wanting to embarrass her, but needing to know if she was in trouble financially. He had to help her, if he could. It was an imperative he didn't understand, but instinct demanded that he heed it.

Her gaze shot up to meet his, a bit of fire returning to her expression. "That's really none of your business."

She made to turn away, but his hand shot out, grasping her upper arm as gently as he could to stop her from fleeing. "I'm sorry, Beth. I just…"

He let her go and moved away, realizing he was probably scaring her. That's the last thing he wanted to do. Thankfully, Tina was somewhere in the back of the bakery and hadn't witnessed any of this part of their conversation.

"I can help you," Trevor tried again. "If you need it." He could feel her drawing away, and he didn't like it.

"My pod is helping me," she answered stiffly as she turned and started walking toward the door of the bakery.

Trevor saw Tina poke her head out from behind one of the ovens, and he waved to let her know they were leaving. He had to catch up to Beth, who was already at the door. When he heard the little bell above the door chime, he knew he was out of time. He had to straighten this out.

Trevor left the bakery and caught up with Beth a short way down the street. Unsurprisingly, she was headed toward the boathouse. He figured she would probably change there and then enter the water and stay there for the night. If he didn't fix things between them before then, he'd have to wait until morning, since there was no way he'd ever find her if she got into the water now.

"Let me apologize, Beth," he said quietly as he matched his steps to hers. She moved fast when she wanted to, even on land.

"No need," she replied tersely, still walking. He fell into step beside her.

"Look, honey, I didn't mean to insult you or pry. I just want to make sure you have what you need to get by." He sighed. He'd never really been good at the emotional stuff that women seemed to excel at.

She stopped short and turned to look at him. "Why?"

"Because I care about you." He hadn't been prepared for her question, so he'd said the first thing that came to mind.

She seemed as shocked as he was by his words. Their gazes caught and held for a timeless moment, and then, as if drawn together by some unseen force, they moved closer…and closer…until finally, she was in his arms, and their lips joined.

The kiss was unlike anything he'd experienced before. There was something sweet and poignant about having Beth in his arms, kissing her lips. It was innocent and, yet, carnal at the same time. It was as if light poured down upon him—through him—a light of purity and passion that he'd never experienced before with any other woman.

She tamed his wildness. She calmed his inner beast. She soothed his soul.

Breathing hard, he let her go. The emotion whirling through him was too much to take in. Too much to understand in a single moment, though somehow, it felt as if his entire life had just changed.

He'd have to think about this... Later.

Right now, he had to get away from her to sort through what had just happened, but he couldn't just leave her standing there on the street. He had to see this thing through and escort her to the boathouse, where she could enter the cove in safety.

Luckily, she seemed as stunned as he felt, and she didn't object when he put his arm around her shoulders and guided her toward the other side of the street, where the boathouse waited in the growing dark. They didn't speak as he escorted her into the building. There were a few of her people around, most heading for the water at this time of night, so Trevor paused with her at the door to the locker rooms.

"Will you be all right from here?" he asked, unable to help himself. An instinct was driving him to see to her safety, and it would not be denied.

She smiled faintly. "I'm with my people. I'm fine. Thanks for dessert." She looked downward, seeming to be a bit shy.

He couldn't resist. He tipped her chin upward with his thumb and brushed a soft kiss across her startled lips.

"Goodnight, sweetheart. Rest well." He drew away, holding her gaze. "I'll see you tomorrow."

He left her there, watching from outside the door until she joined two other mer women on their way into the locker room. She'd be all right with them, he reassured himself. Much as he wanted to go with her right to the water's edge, he knew he couldn't. Not yet. Maybe not ever.

He had to carefully consider how wise it was to get even more deeply involved with her. After all, his life was in Wyoming, and on the road with the Wraiths. He didn't really have room in his current way of life for a female of any kind, much less a mermaid who probably needed to be by the shore at all times. He didn't think any mer would willingly move to a Wyoming mountaintop where there wasn't even a large pond to swim in.

Trevor didn't know how this was all going to play out, but his inner bear didn't want to hear why it wouldn't work. No, the bear was all about making the mermaid his, whatever the circumstances. The bear was getting downright possessive over her, and Trevor's human side wasn't that far behind.

It had all happened so fast. He hadn't intended to get involved with Beth, but the more he saw of her, the more he wanted. She intrigued him on every level and brought out all his protective instincts.

Trevor went back to his hotel, walking along the side of the street closest to the beach. He kept looking out to the waters of the cove, hoping to catch a glimpse of Beth. He knew it was crazy, but the bear inside him whined, wanting to be near her again.

Soon, he placated himself. They'd be together soon.

Trevor filed his report, using his phone to take images of the sketches he'd made and send them along. He thought his superiors would be pleased with what he'd learned so far. Nothing was actionable at this point, but Trevor knew from all his years in the field that time spent gathering first-hand intel was never wasted. The more they knew about the enemy, the better off they'd be when the final confrontation occurred.

He'd already learned more in one day of

swimming with Beth than he had since he'd been here. Tomorrow, he hoped to capture the first video and still images of the creatures. All in all, things were progressing nicely. He'd renewed and strengthened friendships among the founders of Grizzly Cove, and he'd begun to make friends and connections among the mer, as well. So far, so good.

Now, if only he could figure out what he was going to do about Beth. He was very much afraid he was beginning to have deep feelings about her, and he wasn't sure where they would lead. Things could get tricky fast, and for once in his life, Trevor didn't have a plan. Goddess help him.

CHAPTER SEVEN

Beth wasn't keen on the small boat Trevor had procured for their voyage to the mouth of the cove the next day. She always felt like a fish out of water—pun intended—when she was riding on top of the waves, rather than when she was navigating the currents on her own. It just felt weird.

Her senses weren't as sharp in her human shape, above water. She didn't know yet how they were going to manage to deploy the various pieces of equipment. Trevor hadn't really shared his plans with her. She wasn't sure if that meant she was just along for the ride, or if she would have some part to play in gathering the information he was trying to capture on film and video.

Some of the gear looked as if it was designed to be used by a diver, but she hadn't asked too many questions, and Trevor had seemed preoccupied with just getting the boat into position. They were very near the ward's magical barrier now. She could sense it, but not as well as when she was beneath the surface.

"This should be close enough," Trevor said, as if to himself, shutting off the small engine at the rear of the boat and dropping a small anchor over the side.

"Will that be enough to keep us from drifting?" she asked, worried.

"It should be fine. I've used this same kind of equipment many times before," he reassured her, his tone filled with confidence yet easygoing.

"Is everything going to be done from the surface? Or will one of us have to get wet? If so, I volunteer." She held her hand up eagerly as he chuckled.

"You really don't like being on the water instead of in it, do you?"

She touched her finger to the tip of her nose, nodding, to indicate he'd hit it right on the nose. Everything about this made her nervous. And, to make matters worse, the creatures were already acting up. Long tentacles reached out of the ocean just beyond the mouth of the cove, as if waving a sinister hello.

She pointed over Trevor's shoulder, unable to speak for a moment. He turned quickly and cursed, reaching for a camera. He got off a few still shots in rapid succession before the sea monsters disappeared below the surface once more. She'd seen disturbances in at least three distinct areas beyond the ward, and spied tentacles of two separate creatures, if she judged correctly.

"Damn. They're in a mood today, aren't they?" he asked, turning back to smile at her. "Here. Take some photos if you see anything else while I set the rest of this up, okay?"

She took the camera from him, nodding. This wasn't going to be a pleasure cruise. She'd known that from the moment they had set off from the dock. This was a fact-finding mission. It was *work* for him. For her, it was just fear and nerves competing for precedence while she tried to help him and keep them both from straying over the safe zone of the ward.

The noonday sun was high overhead, but it was playing hide and seek with some puffy white clouds, affording them a bit of shade now and again as Trevor set up his gear. Beth kept an eye out for the creatures, but they stayed under the surface while he worked, only showing a roiling tentacle just breaching the surface now and again, which wasn't really enough to take a photo of, in her opinion.

"Looks like there are more of them out there today than usual," she said, watching the water nervously.

"Do you think the boat attracted them?" he asked offhandedly, as if it didn't really matter to him one way or the other. She knew better. He was taking in all the data, all the time. Spending time with him had made her realize there wasn't much that got past his keen observation.

"Probably." She tried to be as nonchalant as him, even though her gut was stirring with a low-pitched dread. She really didn't like being this close to the creatures without her trident.

"I'm sorry, Beth." The soft tone of his words startled her gaze up to his. He was looking at her with gentle concern that touched her heart despite the tense situation. "I didn't realize. This probably brings back bad memories."

She frowned, trying to follow his reasoning. "Memories?"

"Of your flight into the cove on Drew's fishing boat," he said in that caring tone of his that somehow touched an answering sympathetic chord inside her that she hadn't known existed. But his words made her shake her head and smile, just a bit.

"No, this situation is nothing like that," she told him. "Well, not much like it at any rate. I just don't like being so close to so many of those creatures. It reminds me of what came before Drew's arrival, when we were fighting them. Swimming for our lives, turning to make a stand, swimming again. Doing our best to avoid their thrashing tentacles and worse—their teeth." She gazed into the distance as she remembered those horrible moments. "And then, Sirena and some of the others took a stand, going toe to toe with those things. I was powerless to do much of anything except strike out when a tentacle swept too near. I managed to injure quite a few of those reaching arms, but it wasn't enough. We all knew we were going to die there, that day."

"But then, Drew showed up with his boat and his magic," Trevor continued her story, prompting her.

"Yes. If not for him, we would have been leviathan chow. I have no doubt about that." She looked down at the floor of the boat, unable to watch the roiling horizon a moment longer. "Up to that point, I'd been feeling stronger—as if I could stand and fight just about anything in the water. But the leviathan and its smaller friends proved just how delusional I was. I'm as weak as Jonathan always said." That last bit came out as a pained whisper, and the moment she said the words, she regretted uttering them. She'd said too much. Been too honest.

Beth hid her face in her hands, crouching over her knees as she sat on the wooden plank that acted as s seat on this end of the small boat. A moment later, she felt the boat sway as Trevor joined her on the wide seat. He sat next to her and draped his arm around her shoulders, sheltering her. He felt so safe and warm. She wanted to cuddle into his side, but she couldn't. She'd already shown her weakness too much. She had to at least try to salvage some of her pride.

"It's all right, honey," he said in an understanding tone, stroking the skin of her upper arm gently. "There's always a point in a warrior's life where they meet something bigger and meaner than themselves. You have to be pretty tough if it took a sea monster to bring you to that point."

His words were a shock to her system. He saw her as a warrior? Was he joking?

She looked over at him, turning her head to the side to assess his expression. She found he was serious. No hint of humor played around his lips or eyes. Instead, she saw respect and understanding there, which stunned her to her core.

"I'm a coward," she said, unable to hide her true feelings when he was being so kind. "My stepfather bullied me and had me cowed for years until I finally escaped him. I'm not a warrior. I ran from him. I didn't stand and fight."

Trevor's expression didn't change. "Sometimes, retreat is the better part of valor. Making foolish stands against a superior force isn't smart, and it'll get you killed. Think of it this way—you chose retreat so as to better prepare yourself for a future confrontation. What have you been doing since you left home? You asserted your independence. You joined Nansee's pod, and not only did you find a greater force that could protect you—your pod— but you also became a hunter and sought to learn how to fight to protect the pod, as well." He paused, but not for long.

"You took, but you also gave," he went on. "You took the protection, training and camaraderie that you needed, and in return, you gave of yourself to protect the group. I'd say that marks you as a warrior, Beth, even if you don't think so. I've known fighting men who weren't as successful as you've been when the chips were down. Don't ever think less of yourself for doing what you needed to do to survive, regroup and come back stronger."

Beth was floored. He saw her that way? He really thought her actions were proactive instead of just fear-inspired running with no clear destination in sight? Was he stupid or something?

No. Wait. She knew for a fact that Trevor wasn't stupid. In fact, he'd impressed her with his keen mind and powers of observation.

But why would he lie to her?

Maybe he wasn't lying. Maybe he was telling her the way he saw it. Maybe his point of view was objective, not clouded by the swirling emotions of fear and anguish that had plagued her for so long.

He bumped into her side in a playful way. "You still in there?" he asked, bending his head, trying to seek her gaze, which had fallen to the floor of the boat again.

"I'm here," she croaked, her voice a bit unsteady as her thoughts whirled. "I just don't understand how you can see me that way," she admitted.

"Honey…" He turned her on the seat so that she was facing him, then tilted her chin up so he could meet her gaze. "I honestly think you're one of the bravest people I know."

The moment stretched between them, and intimacy forming on that tiny boat in the open air, narrowing her world down to just the space between them. Mere inches separated their lips, and then… He kissed her. A slow, gentle, sweet kiss that quickly morphed into something stronger, hotter, and more devastating than any kiss she'd ever experienced.

Kissing Beth was like a dream come true, and Trevor almost lost his sense of place and timing, but the splash of water against the hull of the boat shook him out of the reverie kissing Beth had caused. He let her go, coming up for air himself, taking stock of where they were. Their little boat was still anchored in safety, behind the ward, but he noted a new presence in the water, watching them with amusement.

"I believe one of your friends has come to visit," Trevor told Beth, noting the way her eyes were wide and dilated with pleasure. A little thrill ran though him, knowing he'd put that look on her face.

Beth straightened and looked around, a sudden blush staining her cheeks when she spotted the mermaid watching them from a few yards away. Laughter preceded the mer woman as she swam slowly toward them. Her face and shoulders were human looking, but as she grew closer, Trevor could just see that she was scaled below the surface of the water, retaining her tail and ability to swim like a fish. That was some trick those mer had, doing partial shifts so easily.

"Don't let me interrupt," the woman said

as she drew closer.

"Stop it, Marla," Beth said, sounding both annoyed and embarrassed.

"Aren't you going to introduce me to your friend, Bethy?" Marla smiled, and Trevor thought the grin was a tad predatory. He watched Beth's reaction with interest, noting the way she seemed to bristle. Was she jealous? Now, wouldn't that be interesting?

"You know perfectly well this is Trevor Williams. Did Nansee ask you to check up on us?" Beth replied, challenge in her every word.

Marla's head tilted as her smile turned sly. "She might've mentioned that you'd be out this way in a boat during my patrol," she admitted. "Is there anything I can do underwater for you, or is this strictly a surface mission?"

"I plan to dive a bit as soon as I've set up the underwater gear," Trevor answered in a friendly tone before Beth could run off the other mermaid. "I'm going to take video of the creatures, so unless you want to be immortalized on film, you might want to stay behind the camera and out of the frame."

"Thanks for the warning. I'm definitely

not ready for my close-up, Mr. DeMille," Marla joked with him, and Trevor noted Beth's attitude with satisfaction. If he wasn't misreading the signs, she definitely was jealous.

He didn't want to toy with her emotions, but he was pleased by the positive sign that he was having an impact on her. Beth was so cagey, never really letting him know for certain what she was thinking. He had to do a lot of guesswork with her, and his inner bear's fur got ruffled at the lack of conclusive evidence that she was as interested in him as he was in her. The show of jealousy calmed the bear, but Trevor wouldn't let Beth think he had any interest whatsoever in her friend. He wouldn't give Beth any cause to doubt his seriousness when it came to what he wanted from her.

His sweet Beth, and no other.

"I'm sure we'll be fine. Marla, was it? Thanks for stopping by," Trevor said, friendly enough, but sending the definite message that he wasn't interested.

He saw the mermaid shrug as she grinned. "I'll be on my way, then. Good hunting to you both."

"Thanks," Trevor replied easily. "And to

you."

Marla dove and swam off without further comment, and Trevor wisely decided to retreat to the equipment while giving Beth time to calm down. He had some neat gizmos that had arrived that morning. Some of it was stuff he'd heard of but never seen, or stuff he'd used a few times while in the service, but was much too costly for him to own himself. It certainly looked like Nansee and John had called in more than a few favors to get such professional equipment here on such short notice. Trevor promised himself he'd make the most of it.

Eventually, Beth calmed and came over to help him unpack some of the gear. Most of the equipment was waterproof, so there had been no advantage to doing the small amount of assembly work on shore. He'd wanted to get out here as fast as possible so as to maximize his time on, and in, the water.

He dove in human form, and she followed him into the water, leaving her clothing in the boat and shifting as soon as she hit the water. He let her trail behind him, his silent shadow, as he used the high-tech gear to get as many shots as possible of the creatures that swam some distance away.

Zoom lenses allowed him to get close-ups, though they were made murky by the amount of water between them. Still, these images would reinforce the sketches he had made of the various types of creatures.

He'd have to do a couple more sketches, though. There were more of the smaller monsters visible today than there had been the last time. Trevor was careful to note the differences between them—the variation in tentacle length and position, as well as the quantity of teeth and their locations. The shapes of the monsters varied slightly, as did their visible displays of aggression.

Trevor caught it all on film, as much as possible. He'd supplement with his drawings as soon as he got back on shore. He'd have quite the report to file. As far as anyone knew, these were the first recorded images of the leviathan's minions that anyone had been able to capture.

They would be kept secret, he knew. The world at large couldn't be exposed to the reality of evil sea monsters patrolling the coast. At least, that was the goal. They were doing everything they could to end this problem before humanity became aware of exactly what was going on. If that happened, nobody could really predict how modern society would react.

It could easily become open season on anything magical. Humans had come a long way since the days of knights and armor when their offensive capabilities had been limited to bows and arrows, swords and pikes. Today, there were laser-guided weapons, heat-seeking missiles and nukes to contend with. Who knew what the human reaction would be to learning about magical creatures living among them?

He worked underwater for an hour at least, coming up for air as needed, Beth a watchful guard and companion at his side. Eventually, it was time to return to the surface, and he chivalrously motioned for Beth to precede him into the boat, giving her time to shift and dress before following her. He busied himself taking a few more photos of the surface when a couple of tentacles showed in the air just across the barrier, but essentially, he'd gotten what he'd come for. It was time to go back. Weighing anchor, he turned the boat back toward shore.

He didn't really want their time together to end. They'd worked well, side by side, and he had enjoyed her company more than he thought possible, even while he worked. Her insights into the creatures and suggestions for capturing the best images had been helpful, and he already planned to give credit where credit was due, when he made his report that evening. One thing was certain, the images he had captured today were going to make a splash—no pun intended. Even Trevor was surprised by the size, quantity, and differing attributes of the creatures he had filmed. There were a lot more of them than he had thought, and in horrifying varieties.

As they approached the shoreline, Trevor knew he had to speak. He had tentative plans for later, which all depended on Beth's response to a question he hadn't yet asked. *Now or never, Trevor.*

"What are you doing for dinner?" He did his best to sound coolly casual.

Beth looked surprised. Pleased, he thought, but surprised.

"I hadn't made any plans," she told him in a tone he could just barely hear above the sound of the outboard motor.

"Would you like to join me for a picnic on the beach tonight? Sort of my way of thanking you for your help today," he explained.

Her eyes lit from within, giving him hope. "Okay," she said, again in that quiet tone he had to strain to hear.

He brought them into the dock just then, busy with the work of shutting down the motor and securing the equipment. Beth worked with him, helping where she could, especially in off-loading the delicate camera bags and boxes onto the dock.

As they made their way to shore after tying up the boat, he took the bulk of the bags, but she insisted on helping. Only then did he bring the matter of dinner back up for conversation. He had big plans, and he didn't want to scare her off by sounding too eager.

"Do you want to meet just before sundown? Is that too late to eat?" he asked, very willing to accommodate her if she didn't like that idea. Tonight was all about putting her more at ease with him.

"That sounds good. I have a few things I have to do in town this afternoon, but I can meet you around sunset. Where?"

"How about we meet at the boathouse and go from there. It's only a short walk to the spot I have in mind." Things were falling perfectly into place, but he dared not take anything for granted.

She agreed, and they parted when they reached the street. Beth handed him the two small bags she'd carried to that point, and he added them to his own load. He had a lot of work to accomplish before he could set his dinner plans into motion. Eager to get started, Trevor headed for his hotel room.

He had two separate missions this afternoon. First, he had to put the images he'd captured into some kind of order and send them to his superiors. At the same time, he had to set a few balls in motion for his second target—dinner on the beach with Beth. If all went well, he'd finish with his report just in time. He'd be cutting it close, but he'd always been pretty good with planning and logistics. He'd make it work.

Beth wasn't sure what to make of Trevor's invitation, but she wasn't going to say no to spending more time with him. She'd tried to stay away, but he intrigued her on such a base level that she couldn't really find it in her to steer clear, despite her misgivings.

He was handsome in a way that stole her

breath. Considerate. Kind. She knew he was a military man and a warrior, but somehow, his imposing stature and martial skills didn't seem threatening. On any other man, she'd be running in fear, but from Trevor? Never. Or...not anymore, at least.

She wanted to spend time with him. Something about her dared her to step outside her hard-won comfort zone and take a chance. Dinner wasn't normally considered a dangerous activity, but she'd never really been on a date. Jonathan hadn't allowed her to experience the same things her contemporaries did. He hadn't let her grow up in anything close to a normal way.

She'd had tutors. She hadn't been allowed to attend a regular school. She'd been denied the social interaction of kids her own age ever since going to live at Jonathan's compound. She'd been allowed to shift and swim under strictly controlled circumstances, with Jonathan and his goons swimming all around her and her mother, keeping them in line and away from anything resembling freedom.

He'd said it was to keep them safe, but Beth had realized it was a prison. Even if her mother had refused to see it.

But she was free from Jonathan's influence here. With the pod, she had learned to live a life independent of threats and fear...for the most part. The only threats were those of the open ocean, and the only fear came from within. Beth had been doing her best to learn how to deal with those more normal things, day by day, until the leviathan and its friends had shown up in their ocean.

All hell breaking loose was an apt description. Now, they were all huddled into the cove, under protection of the bears and the permanent wards put in place by the Alpha bear's *strega* mate. Beth shuddered to think what would have happened without this safe haven.

And now, Trevor was challenging her fragile grasp on her emotions. He'd scared her at first, but she was slowly coming to crave his presence. She had been attracted to him from the beginning, despite herself.

She'd been so set on being negative and seeing only what had been lost that she'd spent a lot of her time in Grizzly Cove pushing people away. She'd been miserable, in fact, until that moment Trevor had walked up to her while she was sitting on that rock, feeling sorry for herself.

It was as if he'd changed everything with just his smile. The sun had come out, and she'd begun to realize just what a sour puss she'd become. The fact that they were essentially stuck in Grizzly Cove until the leviathan was dealt with was bad, but it could've been so much worse.

At least in Grizzly Cove, there was no Jonathan. No threat of danger to her mother if she didn't behave. No fear of beatings that never left a visible mark so she had no evidence to show of the pain and anguish she'd endured at the hands of her so-called stepfather.

No, there were *bears* here. Big, strong, *protective* bears, who had taken her and the entire pod under their wing, so to speak. The bears made the rules, and she knew in her heart that they wouldn't let anything bad happen in their town without doing something about it.

And there was the pod. They knew all about Jonathan and Beth's mother. They wouldn't let anything happen to Beth in the water, or on the land, if they could help it either.

Beth had strong allies now. She wasn't a

scared girl, trying to stand against a shark and his friends on her own. She had grown so much in the years since she'd escaped Jonathan, and she would never go back to being the frightened girl who had nearly disappeared under the force of Jonathan's will.

Never.

CHAPTER EIGHT

Beth met Trevor for dinner, unsure what his beach picnic might imply, but willing to see where it led. She was feeling adventurous and willing to take a risk. That was a mood she hadn't been in for a while, and she welcomed the little spurt of bravery. Jonathan had tried to crush her free will, but every now and then, she found the courage to step outside the small box he'd made for her and try something wild.

That seemingly un-crushable sense of adventure had pushed her to run away and seek the safety of the pod. It had made her try her hand at being a hunter, when staying safely hidden with the bulk of the pod would have been the more prudent course. And now, it was leading her toward a man...a bear shifter...who was unlike any other man she'd ever known.

He was certainly as tough and scary as the men in her past. Those hard-eyed mercenaries had been her stepfather's thugs. They hadn't been allowed to touch her, but they'd looked at her, and just their glances made her feel soiled. They weren't nice men. Not like the gentle giants she'd met since coming to Grizzly Cove. And especially the kind-hearted Trevor.

Trevor greeted her with a smile and walked by her side toward a spot on the beach that wasn't quite visible from the road, but it wasn't so hidden that she felt isolated or afraid. He had a small hibachi grill set up, the coals already glowing a cheery red-orange. Some kind of fish wrapped in tin foil on top of the grill was giving off the most delicious aroma. Salmon, she thought. Yum.

"This is much fancier than I expected," she said as he motioned for her to take a seat on the soft blanket he'd spread over the sand.

"Well, I couldn't serve you take-out

sandwiches," he said, grinning as he turned to check on the portable grill. "And I do have a few recipes that turn out well enough to cook for other people. This salmon is one of them. I hope you don't mind cooked fish."

"Mind?" She laughed. "I love fish in all its variety. In mer form, it's always raw, but when I'm on land, I love the way human chefs find different ways to season and cook it. Whatever you've got going on over there smells absolutely scrumptious."

The meal was as good as its appetizing aromas, and they ate from paper plates while sitting on the shore, watching the waves. And it wasn't just fish. He'd packed a salad and some tasty side dishes. They talked about the town and the people in it. Pleasant conversation. Nothing too deep, which suited her just fine.

Something was happening here, between them. Something almost electric in the air was drawing her closer to him. They sat on the blanket, facing the water, the shushing lap of the wavelets a pleasant background sound. Even though they were on the open beach, they were situated in such a way that it would be hard for anyone from town to see them.

Public, yet private…and perfect for what she had in mind.

The night deepened all around them, the only light the soft red glow of the dying coals, and the bright pinpoints of the stars in the heavens. They were all alone…yet surrounded by life everywhere. Beth's people were settling in for sleep in the cold embrace of the cove waters while, all around in the woods, night creatures prowled, and the good folk of Grizzly Cove settled in for their night shifts—either hunting, sleeping or protecting the cove and all who lived there.

On the beach, it was just the two of them, isolated in their togetherness, under the stars. Beth felt closer to Trevor than she'd been to any man, and she wanted to experience all there was to feel between a man and woman. For once in her life, she wanted to be free of constraints and expectations. Free from worry and anxiety. Free to just feel and enjoy.

She thought she could do that with Trevor. She trusted him enough to think he might just be the one man she could be with who would expect nothing in return but her company. There would be no strings leading back to her stepfather. No political maneuvers. No business deals.

With Trevor, she very much thought what you see was what you get. It was comforting to know he was genuine. He might be scary—the Wraiths hadn't earned their reputation by being gentle—but she also believed he would never use his skills against her. At least not without good reason. And an *honorable* reason.

Trevor might be employed as a mercenary, but he had honor. She truly believed he wouldn't betray her to Jonathan for any amount of money or power. She didn't know why she felt so strongly about this particular point, but she did. He wouldn't betray her. She knew it deep in her soul.

As for where this night might lead, she didn't want to think about it. She just wanted to live for the moment, for the next few hours, which she hoped she would be spending alone with Trevor. Hopefully, skin to skin, in his arms, his body warm over hers. She wanted that more than she wanted her next breath, but he was taking things slow. Too slow for her nerves.

When he started talking about the

constellations, she leaned closer—ostensibly to follow the line of his pointing fingers as he explained the intricacies of celestial navigation. Or something like that. To be honest, she wasn't really listening.

She was just enjoying being close to him, sharing his heat and drinking in his scent. Her mer side was cold at times, but when it felt the urge to mate, her blood could run as hot as any land shifter. Desire was building in her now, and if he didn't make a move soon, she just might take the initiative. Beth almost smiled, wondering how Trevor would react to being pinned down and ravaged.

As the thoughts blossomed into heated images of them entwined in her mind, she found she couldn't wait any longer. Turning to him, Beth covered his lips with hers, startling him into silence. But he didn't remain startled for long.

Trevor took her up on the kiss and joined in as a full participant after only the slightest moment of stunned hesitation. After that, he didn't take much coaxing—which is to say, no coaxing at all—to lie back on the blanket and let her have her wicked way with him.

It had been so long…and never with a man she respected like this. Oh, she'd had a relationship with one of her stepfather's guards, but only after giving her virginity to the man had she learned that the whole arrangement had been carefully organized by Jonathan. It had been yet another way to keep Beth under his thumb.

The guard had been a young protégé of Jonathan's that he was grooming for a more important position in his organization. Seducing the boss's stepdaughter and keeping her in line had been just another part of the job. Another rung on the ladder of success, as it were.

The minute she'd found out about her lover's duplicity, Beth had begun plotting her escape. She knew her weak-willed mother would never be able to leave Jonathan, but Beth had a shot. Maybe. Letting Jonathan believe she was still happily enjoying her first real romance, Beth had been working toward her own freedom, and when the chance had come, she'd taken it and run with it.

Like she was running with this feeling now. This incredible feeling of joyful rapture…wholesome desire. There was no subterfuge with Trevor. He hadn't been colluding with her stepfather. She was certain he liked her for her, not for what her stepfather could do for him.

It was freeing. And very, very sexy. He made her feel more sure of herself and able to pounce on him and demand what she wanted in a way she never had before. As she was doing now.

She pushed at his clothing, wanting it gone. She kissed him with wild abandon as she squirmed to get closer to him in any way possible. Straddling his hips, she rubbed against him, noting with pleasure the hard ridge of his cock straining against the fabric that separated them.

Too much fabric. It had to go.

Breaking the kiss, she worked her way down his body, her breathing heavy as she labored toward her ultimate goal. She unbuttoned his shirt, placing her lips on his muscular torso as she went. He really was the most beautifully built man. Big as a bear, fit as an athlete, warm and welcoming as she could have hoped for. He heated her sea-cooled skin and made her want to stay on land with him...forever?

The thought made her pause just slightly, but the temptation of his skin was too great to be ignored for long. She kissed her way down his torso, but when she started unbuttoning his pants, he stayed her hand. She looked upward to meet his gaze and found his brown eyes, molten in their intensity, focused on her.

"You keep going, and this is gonna be over before it begins, sweetheart," he said, his voice pitched in a low, sexy drawl that she'd never heard from him before. She liked it.

The rumble of his words sent a delightful shiver down her spine. She couldn't help but smile at him.

"Smile like that at me some more, and we might achieve the same effect," he teased, rolling them over on the blanket until he was on top, his muscular thighs between her upraised knees. She loved the delicious friction of his hardness against her soft spots, even if there was still too much fabric between them.

"I like it when your voice gets all growly," she said, realizing as she spoke that she was no longer afraid of him. Not by a long shot. To her, he was a big ol' teddy bear, not a scary grizzly, though she knew he could be scary to other people. Just not to her. Not anymore.

The simple truth was, she knew in her

heart that he would never hurt her. Not for any reason. He smiled down at her, moving his body against hers in a sultry sway that made her breath catch.

"Well, I like the way you're all soft and warm beneath me. Or on top of me. Or any positions you want, as long as it's next to me," he clarified, looking at her in that sexy way he had.

"I can agree with that," she told him, knowing she was still smiling. She had been since this all started, and she doubted anything could wipe the outward sign of happiness from her face right now. She was too joyful to keep it bottled up inside.

"Do you also agree that we're wearing too many clothes?" he asked, a mischievous light in his eyes.

"Oh, yeah. I totally agree there." She nodded at him, going along wherever he wished to lead her.

"What should we do about it, then?" His gaze narrowed as if he was considering different ways to remove her clothing. She liked that look in his eyes. Really liked it.

"I think we need to get naked," she replied with mock-solemnity, still unable to wipe the smile from her lips, even as they played. She'd never played with a man like this. Never teased at such a moment. Never romped.

Now was the time. This was the man. She was going to have fun, for once in her life, and share some moments she would never forget. She was sure of it.

"You know, I think you're right."

He rose slightly so he could shrug off his shirt, and she watched the movement of his muscles with parted lips. *Oh, yeah.* She wanted to lick him all over.

He lifted onto his knees, helping her sit up so he could rid her of her top, as well. That went quick, but when it came time to remove her bra, he laid her back down on the soft blanket after just undoing the hooks at the back. He looked into her eyes as he lowered the straps over each shoulder, and then, his gaze went to her breasts as he bared them...slowly.

He lowered his head, and suddenly, his lips were there. And there. Right where she wanted them. His tongue teased her excited nipples, and her whole body shivered in delight.

She whimpered when he left, moving down her torso, dragging his lips and tongue over her skin on his way to her waist. When he encountered the waistband of her pants, he paused to trace her skin with feather light touches before removing her pants and panties all in one go.

Her breath caught as he knelt between her legs, spreading them wide. He slid a finger into her wet heat, sliding in and out a few times before adding another finger, stretching her, making her ready to take him and igniting a fire in her blood that had never felt this hot or out of control. She watched him watching her, loving the intensity of his gaze as he rubbed his thumb over her clit, and she came apart.

The small climax hit her out of nowhere, the pleasure intense but short-lived. She wanted more. So much more. And she knew, without a doubt, she would get what she needed from Trevor. Only from Trevor.

He must've taken off his pants while she floated in the mist of ecstasy, because the next thing she knew, he was naked. His cock jutted out proudly as he retook his place between her thighs.

"I'm sorry this is so fast," he said, and only then did she realize his shoulders were trembling just the tiniest bit. He was holding back, needing her as much as she needed him.

"Not fast enough, Trev," she managed to gasp out as she tried to catch her breath. He really was the most amazing man. Nobody— in her admittedly limited experience—had ever made her feel so much, so fast, so intense. Only Trevor.

"Really?" He met her eyes, seeming to search her gaze for the truth in her words. "I feel like I'm rushing you," he admitted, that crooked grin making her desire rise yet another notch.

"Any slower and I'll be jumping you, mister," she told him, loving the way they could talk so freely, so fondly during this most intimate act. She'd never had that before. Sex had been a mostly silent affair for her until now. Until Trevor.

"Let's save that for another time." His devilish expression held promises she would definitely take him up on.

This wasn't going to be a one-time thing. Even now, before they'd actually joined their bodies together, he was planning for future encounters, and she was right there with him. It was so good to know they were on the same page.

"Just do me already," she gasped, putting her heels against his back and trying to draw him closer.

"Well, when you ask so nicely..." He came down over her, his cock zeroing in on the spot that needed him so badly. He bit her lower lip playfully. "I like it when you talk dirty like that, honey. You just poked the bear, and now, the bear is going to poke you." He laughed against her lips as he took her mouth in a potent kiss.

At the same time, he was pushing in below, gentle at first, seeming to gauge her comfort level as he went along. He was a considerate lover who gave more than he took—at least so far. She couldn't wait to turn the tables on him, but for now, this traditional position and possession was just what she wanted for their first time.

He slid in to the hilt, and she thought she might just die of bliss right then and there. He fit her perfectly. As if he'd been made just for her.

The thought occurred... Maybe he had been. Maybe he was the one she'd dreamed of but never thought she'd find. Maybe he was her...mate.

On that shocking thought, he began to

move. Slowly at first, his tempo rose quickly, as did her passion. She'd had a little taste of the pleasure he could bring already, but she wanted it all this time. She wanted him to come with her, burying himself deep in her body while she quaked in delight.

She wasn't worried about consequences. Mer were notoriously hard to conceive, and she knew shifters didn't carry diseases the way humans could. There was nothing to stop them from enjoying each other with no holds barred, so to speak, which was good considering the thirst she had developed for this surprising bear shifter.

A thirst that seemed unquenchable in this lifetime, but she'd spend the rest of her life happily trying. If he felt the same.

And then, suddenly, it was real. She knew she wasn't playing around with Trevor. The indefinable something about him that had attracted her from the get go resolved into the certain knowledge that he was the closest she'd ever come to meeting her mate.

Sweet Mother of All. In all probability, he was it. Her mate.

The next few minutes should prove the point one way or another. Shifters often recognized their mates after having sex for the first time. Some knew before, and she'd heard that some took longer, but she figured she'd be right in the middle. If he blew her mind and rocked her world the way she thought he would, she'd never be the same again after this climax.

It was both a scary thought and one she cherished. Some shifters went all their lives without ever coming close to true mating. The lucky ones found their mates young and spent all their years side by side.

Beth wasn't sure what was going to happen here, but she was open and willing in a way she hadn't ever thought she'd be. In this amazing moment with the man she'd come to admire like no other pounding into her receptive body, she wanted him to be the one.

And then, there wasn't any more time for thought as Trevor's pace changed. He shifted just slightly, altering the angle of penetration and hitting some heretofore unknown spot inside her that made her want to scream. She couldn't, of course. They were on the beach where screams might bring people running, but she wanted to. Instead, she clutched at his shoulders, her nails sinking into his flesh as he strained above her.

"Come on, Beth. I can't hold it together much longer. Come for me now, baby," he chanted, his words puffing against her skin in hot panting breaths.

She moaned as she came, unable to bite back the sound that might betray them to passersby, but she didn't really care. Not then. Not while her world was being blown apart and put back together again by one man. Trevor.

Her mate.

They lay side by side under the stars for a while, not talking, just enjoying the moment and catching their breath. Beth wasn't sure if Trevor had been as deeply affected as she'd been by their joining, and she was a bit too shy and uncertain to ask. She didn't want to wreck the mood by saying something wrong, so she just kept her own counsel.

"I was going to say something about how those pretty stars up there had nothing on you, but the minute I touched you, I was lost," Trevor admitted on a sigh. "I was trying to be all Joe Cool, and instead, I turned into Speedy Gonzalez." He turned to face her, lying on his side on the blanket. He was nude. Deliciously so. "I'm sorry, honey." He put a hand on her waist and rubbed his thumb over her skin in an almost hypnotic way.

She had to chuckle. "Do you hear me complaining, Speedy? I was right there with you. In fact, you could've gone a lot faster, and I'd have been more than okay with it."

He smiled, gazing deep into her eyes. "Well... If you're sure. But will you give me another chance to prove the name Speedy should never become my nickname?" He laughed as he lowered his head to blow a gentle raspberry on her shoulder. Then, he kissed it, melting her heart as he looked up at her from beneath his thick eyelashes.

Damn. The man was just too appetizing for words.

"Come back to the hotel with me tonight. Stay with me and let me make love with you again, Beth. Once is just not enough." He kissed his way over her collarbone as she sucked in a breath. He was seduction itself, but he didn't have to say much to get her agreement. She'd wanted to extend this night as much as she could, anyway.

It all might go to hell tomorrow, but at least she'd have tonight. That's the way she looked at it. That's the way life had forced her to look at things for too many years to count.

"I like the sound of that," she whispered as he lifted his head, blocking out the stars.

"I'll make sure you don't regret it," he promised, and then, he kissed her again. The stars were behind her eyes as he woke passions she'd thought would remain dormant for a little while longer.

CHAPTER NINE

A short while later, Beth went with Trevor to his hotel, and they made love long into the night. She was left in no doubt that Trevor was her mate, but he remained stubbornly silent on the topic, and she refused to say anything to ruin the stolen night in his arms. If this was all she'd ever have of bliss, she wasn't going to make it end with foolish words.

Trevor was a rolling stone. A mercenary who traveled a lot, risking his life repeatedly. He wasn't exactly a stable sort of man, and she doubted he wanted to be tied to a mate, regardless of how good they were together.

One thing Beth was grateful for was that she finally understood why her friends had given up the hunting party and their ocean-going ways to mate with their bear shifters. She truly hadn't understood the pull a mate could have on a woman.

Beth thought she just might give up everything if Trevor would only ask her to be his forever. Oh, she wasn't holding her breath, waiting for that. She hardly expected it. He didn't seem the settling-down kind of man. Not at all. But if he did... She would give him everything in a heartbeat and never look back.

As her friends had done for their bear shifter mates.

She fell asleep in his arms and dreamed of a cabin by the shore where they could live together forever. It was a nice dream, but only that...a dream.

Beth woke before Trevor and realized, in the darkness of predawn, that there was no hope for them as a couple. He was a mercenary who lived on a mountaintop. There was no way she could thrive in an environment like that. He also traveled a lot, and she had major limitations in that she had to be near the water. Coastlines were her domain. Not mountains or anyplace inland, for that matter. Most of the world was inland. A guy like Trevor wouldn't easily be able to live with such prohibitions.

Oh, it had been a beautiful dream in the middle of a passion-filled night, but in the cruel glow of predawn, things were much clearer. When her head wasn't filled with the mind-numbing pleasure of Trevor's caresses, harsh reality reared its ugly head. It could never work between them. She'd been fooling herself entertaining any idea that it could.

Heart breaking, she slid out of bed and to the door, not even bothering with her clothing as she ran down the beach and straight into the sea. The hotel was on the beach side of the main road, and Trevor's room faced the water, so there was little chance anybody would see her this early, in the dark, going into the water and not coming out again.

She swam as if her life depended on it, running from her sorrow, as she'd run from all the problems in her life. She couldn't face Trevor in the morning light. Not after the night they'd just spent. She needed some time alone, in the water, to clear her head and rebuild her courage to face him again.

After bearing her soul to him in the depths of their stolen night, she would have to gird herself with steely determination to keep from begging him to love her and mate with her the next time she saw him. Beth wouldn't do it. She had more pride than that. But her heart would break, and so, she needed the solace of the water in order to prepare herself for the ultimate heartache…rejection from her true mate.

She knew it was coming. She just didn't want to see it in his eyes this morning.

Goddess help her, she wanted to believe in the dream for a little while longer.

Trevor woke when she left the bed, but she was a quick little thing. He'd never expected her to make a run for it. He followed, but she was already down the beach and into the water before he could catch up with her.

He wanted to bellow. He wanted to rage. But he knew it was no use getting angry. He was a soldier. He'd come up with a plan of action, and then, he'd execute his plan…and win his mate.

There was no doubt in his mind after last

night that Beth was his true mate. He just had to figure a way to convince her of that simple fact. He had to make her love him and be willing to give up a lot to be with him. Which was a problem.

He knew there were some rather large stumbling blocks to any relationship with Beth. For one, he was still employed by Jesse Moore, who'd been hired by the Kinkaid Alpha. He had a mission to fulfill, and his duty to his longtime CO was clear. He had to finish what he'd started here in Grizzly Cove.

The thing of it was...as soon as he finished gathering what intel could be found here, Moore might very well reassign him someplace else. For the first time in his life, Trevor didn't want to go. He had found something—some*one*—worth staying for.

He wanted to stay with Beth. Regardless of whether or not she could fully accept him as her mate, he wanted to be near her. He wanted to protect her and watch over her. He wanted to watch her bloom into the strong woman hiding just underneath her surface fears.

If Major Moore gave him new orders, Trevor didn't know what he'd do. Quit his job? Quite possibly. But he had no idea what he'd do to earn a living if he didn't work for Moore. Moreover, his current home was in Wyoming, on the mountaintop Major Moore had claimed and set aside for his men. If Trevor ceased to work for the major, would he also have to cease being a member of his Pack? Would he have to move?

And how could he not, with Beth living here and needing the water so desperately? There were lakes in Wyoming, but mermaids needed the ocean, didn't they?

It was pretty clear there would have to be some major upheavals in Trevor's existence to make this mating happen. He hadn't thought it all the way through yet, but given time, he was sure he could figure out a way to make it all work.

The first thing he had to do was talk to Big John. The Alpha bear of Grizzly Cove had a way of making things click. Perhaps, if Trevor laid his situation out for one of the world's top strategists, John could come up with some ideas on how to solve some of the outstanding issues. Certainly, Grizzly Cove was going to be part of the solution if Beth wanted to remain with her pod, so talking to the man in charge of the town and the Clan that lived here was a good first step.

For now, he had to beat a strategic retreat and allow Beth some space. Something had freaked her out and sent her running—literally—into the cove. He hoped it was the same thing that had him in a mental tizzy, but he couldn't be sure. Women were hard to read, and mermaids the toughest of all, he was learning.

But she was safe with her people in the cove for now. He had some plans to make before he could talk to her again and hopefully convince her to stay with him for the rest of their lives.

Hours later, after breakfast and a long discussion with Big John, Trevor's next calls were to Major Moore and the man who was footing the bill for this particular mission, Samson Kinkaid. It had been John's idea to involve Kinkaid, and although Trevor wasn't certain at first, the Alpha bear's strategy paid off in spades.

Armed with new information and a solid plan, Trevor couldn't wait to talk to Beth about the things he'd just set in motion, but he had a few other action items he had to accomplish first. For one, he had to check out some intel Big John had passed along about strangers being spotted in the woods. John had asked Trevor to keep his eyes open, as he had all the former operatives who were now residents of Grizzly Cove.

Some civilians had run across signs of deep-cover surveillance, though they hadn't really recognized it as such. Still, one or two of the non-military residents had called the sheriff, and one had even called John directly. He'd confirmed the vague sightings. There were strangers in the woods, casing the town. Whether or not hostile action was imminent remained to be seen, but everyone had been put on alert, and those with military training—Trevor included—were the first line of defense.

Trevor had readily agreed to help defend the town, should it come to that. Barring direct hostilities, Trevor had vowed to stay alert for anything anomalous, with an eye toward sharing any intel he gathered on those who might be watching the town.

He was only too happy to help. Aside from wanting to keep Beth safe, Trevor genuinely liked the town and its people. He didn't want to see anyone in Grizzly Cove come to harm.

To that end, Trevor decided to spend the

next few hours prowling around in the woods at the perimeter of the town. Beth was on duty, patrolling the ward, and would be—according to Marla—for the next eight hours at least. Apparently, Beth had traded shifts with another patroller to give herself a double shift.

Marla had winked at him when she'd said it, along with wishing him well in his pursuit of her friend. She'd suggested he not let Beth become *the one that got away*, as if she was the main character in some kind of fish story. He supposed that was mermaid humor, but he understood what she'd meant. Marla was giving him tacit approval in his pursuit of her friend. He only hoped the rest of the pod would feel the same.

He thought about that as he prowled through the woods surrounding the town. He was careful to stay clear of other bears' property lines, but he saw a few of the guys and exchanged the silent nod of acknowledgment that meant it was okay that he was so close to their personal territories. John had gotten the word out, and those who could be home, patrolling their own areas, were doing so, Trevor was glad to see.

Anything that threatened the town also

threatened the new inhabitants of the cove, and that was unacceptable, as far as Trevor was concerned. No one would pose a danger to his mate—unclaimed as she was—while he drew breath. It might take some time to convince her that she belonged with him, but Trevor was already thinking in terms of a siege. He would wait and watch, never letting up pressure until finally, one day, she'd agree to be his mate.

She had to. The alternative was also unacceptable.

Trevor frowned as he walked silently through the forest, both at his dark thoughts and the faint trail he had just picked up. He sniffed. Human.

Human, and… There was another scent here too. Masked by a really stinky human overlay, but under it, there was a shifter tang. Something mangy. Wolf? Or perhaps coyote? And something feline. Leopard or maybe even mountain lion. It was hard to tell with the human stink overlaying everything.

That wasn't normal. Humans had a different odor than shifters, of course, but usually, it was related to the heavily scented soaps and perfumes they favored. Under the chemicals, there was a more natural scent—stronger in those that had been sweating, or who hadn't bathed in a while—but this… This was way more pungent than that. This was the reek of a body that hadn't washed in months and lay in its own filth.

It was overpowering and bad enough to almost completely mask the underlying shifter scents. But Trevor remembered this tactic. He'd seen it before. Some less scrupulous shifter mercenary groups used it. As did the occasional shifter bounty hunter.

Trevor frowned as the thought crossed his mind. If shifter mercs were involved, Major Moore might be able to get the inside line. There weren't that many groups like his in operation in the States, and the leadership of each of the units liked to keep in touch so they didn't end up fighting against one another. Shifter mercs had a very different code of honor that humans wouldn't really understand, but it worked for them.

If it was bounty hunters, that was another story. They were much harder to keep track of and pin down, and they weren't organized into units like the soldiers of fortune. Plus, if bounty hunters had been set on Grizzly Cove, they had to have a target. Finding out who might have a price on their heads was going to be an interesting exercise...and a dangerous one. If they didn't figure out who was being hunted in time, things could go downhill very quickly.

Trevor circled back after his trek through the woods and went straight to the sheriff's office. Brody was coordinating the reports of strangers, and Trevor knew he'd be the man to alert about his findings. Brody would escalate it from there. The chain of command was there for a reason, and Trevor respected it.

When he reached the office, he found Nansee there before him, sitting at a conference table at which Big John was also seated. Brody waved him over and gestured for Trevor to join the group. Nansee and John nodded at him, but kept on talking, and when Trevor realized what Nansee was saying, he began to get an itchy feeling between his shoulder blades that was both familiar and terrifying.

Someone was hunting him. But that made no sense. They couldn't be hunting *him*. There was no reason for it. Then, realization dawned. They weren't hunting *him*. They were hunting his *mate*.

"Son of a bitch!" Trevor exclaimed, jumping up from his chair. He began to pace as worry set in.

"What is it?" John asked immediately, a frown marring his brows.

"Nansee's talking about sharks in the water, seeming to cooperate with the minions. Well, hell!" he shouted. "I've just detected bounty hunters in the woods."

"You did?" Brody asked sharply, drawing Trevor's attention.

He was too agitated to calm down, even though he knew he was handling this badly. He hadn't been so shaken since... Well, since ever. Then again, he'd never found his mate before and realized she was in danger.

"That or mercs, but I'd lay money on bounty hunters, considering there are motherfucking *sharks* in the water, playing for the wrong team." Trevor ran his hands through his hair in frustration. "Where's Beth?" he asked Nansee directly.

Nansee figured out what he was getting at right away. He could see the knowledge in her eyes.

"She's safe for now. Minding the children in the heart of our new territory. She'll be there for another few hours." Nansee rose from her seat, a worried look on her face. "I'll pull her from the sentry roster, though I doubt those particular sharks could get through the ward. They're as evil as the other things stalking the boundary. But you never know."

"Good." Trevor nodded.

"Just what's going on here, and what does Beth have to do with it? Is she in danger?" Brody asked, his expression concerned.

Trevor looked at Nansee. "They need to know the details," he said quietly. Nansee seemed to think about it for a few minutes, then nodded.

"Tell them while I go put our people on alert to watch over Beth," she said, already walking toward the door.

When just the three bear shifters were left, Trevor sat back down, laying out what he knew for the other two men. He told them about Beth's stepfather and that he was a shark shifter who surrounded himself with thugs. He relayed his suspicions about how Beth was treated as a youngster and what was almost certainly some kind of warped, abusive relationship between her mother and stepfather.

He also told them about the human odor

trick the bounty hunters were employing to try to hide their scents. John nodded grimly at this report.

"I ran across that tactic once myself in Afghanistan. The shifter in question had rolled some poor homeless human drunkard and stolen his coat. The stench of the filthy thing fouled our trackers' noses, and though the trail was easy enough to follow, it led to an ambush of shifter proportions rather than the drunk human we were expecting. Nearly lost a few of my men on that op because of that trick, so we won't soon forget it."

"I had something similar happen once, but it turned out to be a lone bounty hunter here in the States. He was a grizzly by the name of Ezra Tate. Not a bad sort, as it turned out, but there were some tense moments when I tracked him until we realized we were both after the same guy," Trevor told them.

"What happened?" Brody asked.

"We tracked the target together. I let Ezra take him after I'd interrogated him for the intel my unit needed. My CO didn't care what happened to the bastard after we got what we wanted so there was no conflict in letting Ezra take the bounty." A thought occurred to Trevor. "I'll give him a call. I don't think it's him up there in your woods, but he might know who is and what they've been offered...and for whom."

John stood, his face grim. "Make the call. I don't like the idea of anyone putting a price on the head of someone in my town. We need to get to the bottom of this ASAP."

"Yes, sir." When John spoke in that commanding tone of voice, it was hard to remember that he'd retired from the military.

Beth was grateful that Nansee had taken one look at her and assigned her to guard the children today. She was in no shape to be out there on the boundary, staring down sea monsters. Not after the devastating revelations of the night.

She'd found her mate, but it seemed like everything was stacked against her. Trevor was a traveling man, a soul who didn't really have ties to any one place...except maybe that mountain in Wyoming he'd mentioned briefly. And how was a mermaid supposed to survive in the mountains? Or worse, traveling all the time from one war to another.

That was assuming he'd even want to

acknowledge her as his mate. It might not be the same for him. He might not be feeling what she was feeling—or if he did, he might not want to follow through on it. He probably liked his life just the way it was and didn't have room in it for a clingy female with baggage of her own.

She might never be totally free of her stepfather. As it was, she was always looking over her shoulder when she was on land. Except when she was on the streets of Grizzly Cove, she realized. This place felt safer than any other place she'd been since running away from her stepfather's home.

The bears here made her feel as if nothing, and no one, could get past them to get to her. Even if they didn't know about her problems, they would protect anyone in their territory. She knew that in her heart. And since meeting Trevor, she knew he would be the first one to stand up for her against anyone who might come looking for her.

He knew more about her background than any of the other bear shifters. He knew as much, if not more, than Nansee. Beth had trusted him with her fears and most of the story behind her need to escape to the pod.

During those long hours of the night they'd spent together, she'd told him about growing up on Catalina Island and the gilded cage of a mansion Jonathan owned. She had told Trevor about her mother's weakness for the despicable man she'd married and her seeming willful blindness where his threats to Beth were concerned.

Beth would never understand why her mother hadn't left Jonathan long ago. She wouldn't comprehend how she could let him overrun and control every aspect of their lives. How he could threaten them and still somehow have her mother's loyalty. Beth suspected drugs. Or mind control. Something. There had to be a reason why her formerly sane mother had thrown her lot in with Jonathan—a man as evil as the leviathan, in his way.

He just hid it better. His evil was covered by thousand dollar suits and imported Italian loafers. His cunning only came out in sharp words—and occasionally in his sharp shark teeth, when he shifted, though he'd been shifting less and less as his land empire grew. What good was ruling a territory in the sea if he could rule on land, as well? Jonathan wanted it all, it seemed, and he was well on his way to achieving his goal in the most despicable way possible.

Name a shady sector of society, and Jonathan had his hand in it. Prostitution, human trafficking, drugs. He was up to his eyeballs in it all. His dirty empire had allowed him to amass a fortune, with which he hired more thugs—shifters among them—to keep expanding his reach.

There weren't too many young mer in the pod, but during the day, while their parents were busy on land, setting up homes and arranging for funds, clothing and other items they'd need if they were going to stay here any length of time, the children were gathered together into the deepest part of the cove where they were setting up a village, of sorts. It was the safest place they'd been able to manage so far. Patrols watched the perimeter, and the adults were quickly constructing a maze with the native plants and boulders that would allow only limited access to the most vulnerable places.

Beth was babysitting, for lack of a better word, along with a few of the more maternal females. It was soft duty, but one Beth took seriously. Guarding the young was an important task and one she would never take lightly, even if this duty was meant to help her get her head on straight after the emotional upheavals of the night.

Beth was watching three of the youngsters play when Nansee swam up to her, motioning for the others to take over while she led Beth away and then to the surface where they could talk. They could communicate underwater with a series of gestures that all mer knew, but for times when complex issues were to be discussed, nothing beat good ol' English.

The news wasn't good. Nansee had received reports on her way in that the sharks were testing the ward. A few were making some headway before being repulsed, and that was enough to raise the alarm among the patrollers. The waters of the cove might not be as safe as Beth had thought.

With Nansee's permission and encouragement, Beth headed for land. It might not be any safer up top, but that's where Trevor was, and she knew, deep in her heart, that her mate would do his best to protect her—even if he wasn't up to acknowledging that they were, indeed, mates.

Instinct was screaming at her to go to

him. That the safest place for her was with him. That he would help keep her safe.

Nansee escorted Beth to the boathouse and waited to be sure Beth was all right on land before the pod leader headed back into the water. She had to organize the defense of the cove, should the shark shifters somehow gain entry. Beth understood the priorities that Nansee had to deal with as leader, and she didn't begrudge Nansee's need to leave Beth alone once she'd made landfall.

Beth would find Trevor. That was her goal. He'd know what to do. He was some kind of badass mercenary soldier bear. Fighting on land was his bailiwick. If she could just find him, she couldn't be in safer hands.

And as far as the relationship went, in the light of recent developments, the obstacles in their path didn't seem all that important. When life and death were on the line, little things like where she lived, or whether or not he realized yet that they were meant to be together forever, didn't really matter. All that mattered was being with him.

If the worst should happen, she wanted to be by his side.

The emotional turmoil of the last few

hours was over. With a much clearer mind and fuller heart, she sought her mate.

She decided, then and there, that she would go to Wyoming to live with him, if that's what he wanted, because living without him would be impossible. She'd been in physical pain since leaving him this morning, her heart aching. She had come to the realization—danger crystallizing her thoughts as nothing else could—that she needed him in her life, no matter the cost. She would gladly give up the ocean if it meant being with Trevor.

For a mer, there was no greater sacrifice. No greater token of love.

Now she just had to find Trevor and convince him that they belonged together. She had to be brave and declare her love, hoping that he felt the same way. If he didn't, she would try not to be devastated, she promised herself. No, if he hadn't come around yet, she would be patient and persevere. She would wait for him as long as it took. And yes, she'd accept whatever crumbs of affection he gave her.

She wasn't proud. She would take what she could get. In a life starved of affection, Trevor was like the dawn of the new day. He was hope to her. He was love... Whether he realized it yet, or not.

All she had to do now was find him.

CHAPTER TEN

Trevor's sixth sense was telling him something was wrong even before he hit the far end of Main Street, up by the half-completed hotel where he had been staying. The hotel was on one end of the main part of town, too close to the woods for comfort now that he knew hunters were wandering around loose up there, in all likelihood, searching for his mate.

It wouldn't be safe to keep her there another night. He'd have to find a better place to keep her safe, if she was willing to stay on land with him. He hoped like hell she was, because he thought he just might go bat-shit crazy if she insisted on staying in the water, despite the risk of shark shifter goons coming for her.

For all he knew, a few of those predators had come in on two feet, through the woods, with the bounty hunters. If they were already in town, they could probably slide into the water from the side of the barrier and wreak havoc. Trevor wasn't absolutely certain about that. He'd have to check with the *strega* on exactly how her ward was set up. But for right now, he wasn't taking any chances.

He had to get to Beth and keep her with him on land. Then maybe they could figure out this mating business between them. He had no idea if she was feeling the same pull that he was experiencing, but if he had to, he would wait for her forever. He would protect her with his life, and all his skill. He would put her happiness before his own, and he'd live wherever she wanted.

If she chose the sea instead of him, he'd get as close as he could. He'd buy a beach house on the shore and make it clear to her that she was welcomed there any time, day or night. He'd do whatever it took to make her realize that they belonged together.

The immediate danger was real enough.

Trevor had called his friend, Ezra, and confirmed the bounty that had been put on Beth's head. The only consolation was that it wasn't a dead-or-alive kind of contract. No, the slime ball who had put a price on Beth's head wanted her alive and not *permanently* damaged.

That word irked Trevor. She couldn't be *permanently* damaged, which meant it was okay if she was damaged in the process of capturing her. What kind of fiend put that kind of contract out on his own family? Even if they weren't related by blood, Beth was still Jonathan's stepdaughter. Shouldn't the shark-faced bastard be a little more cautious with her safety?

Ezra just happened to be a couple of hours away, in Oregon, and had volunteered to come up and help Trevor, since the bounty he was hunting had led him to a dead end. Trevor saw the sense in having a bounty hunter's input in chasing down others of his kind. Ezra was a stand-up guy, but many others who found themselves employed in hunting others for money weren't so scrupulous.

Ezra knew most of his competition and could give Trevor the inside track on how they operated. He'd be a great help in this particular situation, and Trevor had convinced Big John, vouching for Ezra with the Alpha bear.

After gaining John's approval for his plan, Trevor went back up into the woods to do some quick recon. Ezra had given him a few things to look for, and Trevor wanted to collect as much intel as possible before his old friend arrived.

He was just on his way down, back to town, when the little hairs at the back of his neck started to itch. He knew that feeling. Something was about to go down, and it wasn't anything good.

Trevor pulled his bowie knife from its sheath as he moved out of the trees and into town. It was the largest blade he wore at the moment, having disarmed for the most part on arriving in Grizzly Cove. It just wasn't done to walk around a civilized town armed to the teeth. But his instincts were telling him now was the time to arm himself if he was going to do so because something was happening...right now.

He didn't have time to stop in his hotel room and get his weapons. The knife and his bare hands would have to do, but he wasn't too worried. Even against shifters, he was known as a fighter to be reckoned with. He didn't engage in hand-to-hand combat as much as he used to, but some skills, once learned, were never completely lost.

Then, he saw them. Five men gathered around a central figure. A *smaller* figure. Oh, hell, they were surrounding Beth, right there at the dark end of Main Street with nobody else in sight.

Son of a bitch!

Trevor was still over ten yards away, but he had to get those bastards away from his mate. He put two fingers to his mouth and let loose with a piercing whistle. Not only would the bounty hunters hear him, but if anyone else was around, they would come along eventually to see what the noise was about. Trevor hoped backup would arrive soon, for Beth's sake, but one glimpse of the terror on her face was enough to fuel his ire.

He'd mop the floor with these bastards regardless of who came out to help...or not. They'd scared his mate, and for that, they were gonna bleed.

They'd all looked up at him at his whistle and were now sizing him up as the front three came forward to meet him. They were working together. Shit. The bounty must be damned high if they were agreeing to pool resources and split the money five ways. That was the one thing Ezra hadn't known off the top of his head. He'd promised to look up the details and have that information for Trevor shortly.

The two in back made a move to grab Beth, one on each side. She shied away from them, and Trevor got even more pissed at the stark look of terror on her face. These bastards weren't just going to bleed. Trevor might just have to kill them.

"Hey, assholes!" he shouted to the goons behind her. "Touch her and you die. You get me?"

The three in front advanced closer, but Trevor noted with satisfaction that the other two merely flanked Beth now, but didn't make a move to grab her. He guessed they were waiting to see which way the fight went before they took the chance. Fine with Trevor. As long as they didn't touch her, he wouldn't kill them. That didn't mean he wasn't going to make them pay for scaring her.

That was the last thought he had before he engaged with the first man. They weren't coming at him one at a time. No, that would be too honorable for scumbags like these. They were ganging up on him, but Trevor didn't give a shit. He would take them all down until no one stood between him and his mate. They didn't know it yet, but the five bounty hunters were all going to need a doctor very soon.

Beth was shaking, surrounded by five big men who were definitely not locals, and most assuredly *not* bears. She knew the scent of bear shifters now, and although these guys smelled of fur, she couldn't place what kind of animal shared their skin. It didn't matter, though, because all five were intent on capturing her and taking her back to Jonathan. One of them had said as much, telling her they were taking her back to her father whether she liked it or not.

She'd told them in no uncertain terms that Jonathan was not her father, but they didn't seem to care. The fact was, Jonathan had put a price on her head high enough to get these goons to come after her, and she was in big trouble. She knew it, and she could do nothing about it, which frightened her most of all.

Then, a piercing whistle filled the air, and the five men around her turned as one to face the woods and the man coming out of them. Bright stars above, it was Trevor. Thank the Goddess!

That thought was followed quickly by fear for his safety. He was a soldier, but there was only one of him against five big shifter men who looked like they knew how to fight. She was worried for herself, but now, she was worried for Trevor, as well.

He said something to the two men who had tried to grab her arms, and they eased off, though they still boxed her in. She guessed they were waiting to see how the fight with the other three went before they laid their hands on her. Beth wished she knew how to fight on land like she did in the sea. She wished she had her trident. She'd gladly stick the pointy forks into the two jerks that penned her in.

She couldn't get away from them, but somewhat to her horror, she had a clear view of the fight going on just a few yards up the street. Three hoodlums were ganging up on Trevor, but he was holding his own. In fact, he was coming out on top.

She'd known he was a soldier, but the

skills he displayed now, fighting three on one in hand-to-hand combat, impressed the hell out of her. He was a blur as he moved from motion to motion. Block to kick, to punch that made her wince as she clearly heard bones cracking. Not Trevor's bones. His opponents.

One by one, they fell to the ground, whimpering in pain, blood flowing from numerous places. She'd always known Trevor was a badass, but when he walked quietly forward, leaving a trail of bodies behind him, the look on his face told her she hadn't even guessed at the full extent of his badassery.

He was unharmed. His hair might be a little mussed, but other than that, he was clean. It was his attackers who were bleeding all over the place.

Trevor strode forward, toward her, and she'd never been happier to see him. Or more impressed. Her mate was a rock star. A soldier who knew how to kick ass when needed and strike fear into the hearts of dominant male shifters everywhere. She would've creamed her panties if she wasn't still shaking in her boots.

"You two want to join your friends?"

Trevor asked the men who were still at her sides. One of them retreated a few feet, but the other pulled a gun out of his waistband and aimed it at Trevor.

Heart in her throat, she watched what she expected to be a standoff. But Trevor wasn't stopping. He kept coming, and the men at her side began to tremble. They were scared! She could smell the fear, even though mer noses weren't as acute as a bear's.

"You pull that trigger, son, you're a dead man. Look around. You take me down, you'll still have to deal with them." Trevor nodded toward a spot behind her and then off to her side.

Beth dared to look and found the man who'd backed off was being held firmly by the deputy sheriff. The mayor and what looked like the entire town council were gathered behind her.

The guy with the gun saw what she saw, his eyes widening in sudden fear. Close up, she thought maybe he was some kind of cat shifter, and he was certainly no match for half dozen bears—some of whom were already showing signs of fur and claws.

Thank the Goddess! The cavalry had arrived.

Not that Trevor couldn't have handled it
on his own. After seeing him in action, she
had no doubt he'd had something up his
sleeve to deal with the cat and his pea
shooter. She'd have to ask him about it—
later—after she had a chance to squeeze him
for all she was worth. He'd saved her.

Not only was he her mate. He was her
hero.

Trevor didn't want to admit how badly
he'd been shaken by seeing his newfound
mate surrounded by those five ruffians.
When the one next to her pulled a gun, he'd
about gone out of his mind. He wanted to
tear the man to pieces, but the other bears
were around her now, and he sensed they
wouldn't approve. This was their town, after
all, and Trevor had to abide by their rules in
their territory.

After the former Special Forces unit led
by John Marshall showed up, the standoff
ended rather abruptly. The jerk with the gun
might be brave enough to challenge one
grizzly, but not an entire team of bears who
had claimed this territory as their home.

Trevor walked right up to the cat shifter
and took the gun out of his hand. He held

the other man's gaze as he expertly popped the clip of ammunition out, then removed the bullet that had been waiting in the chamber. Useless now, with no load of deadly metal inside it, Trevor tucked the handgun into one of his pockets, the ammo going into another. No sense wasting a decent firearm when he still might need all the firepower he could get to protect his mate.

By that time, Brody was there, behind the shaking cat shifter. If not for Brody taking the bounty hunter who had drawn steel on Trevor into custody, things still might have escalated. Trevor was shaking with anger at not being able to pummel the bastard into the ground, but then, he realized Beth was standing just a few feet away. She was shaking too, but not with anger. His poor baby was afraid.

Turning to her, he let the other bears handle cleanup. All that mattered right now was Beth. He trusted that the Grizzly Cove town council—Spec Ops warriors, one and all—would know what to do with five mangy shifter bounty hunters. Trevor went to Beth and took her into his arms. His heart filled with tenderness when she clung to him.

"Come here, sweetheart," he whispered near her ear. "It's over now. You're safe."

She didn't say anything for a long time, and while he was conscious of the other bears working around them, Trevor remained aware of the danger of staying out in the open on the street, but with so many others around at the moment, he figured they were safe enough. Still, he wanted her off the street, somewhere safe—or someplace that he could make safe.

That thought in mind, he realized the half-finished hotel might work better than he'd thought earlier, especially now that the bounty hunters would be at the other end of town, in the jail. With the assistance of John and his team, Trevor could make his hotel room into a mini-fortress. And when Ezra arrived, he'd need a place to sleep.

The room next to Trevor's was open and ready. Trevor knew his old friend wouldn't object to adding his own layer of protection by setting himself up in that room. He'd already volunteered to help in any way he could, and Trevor knew Ezra well enough to be certain that if he gave his word, he wouldn't go against it, even if it meant passing up a huge bounty.

Unlike most in his profession, it wasn't *all* about the money for Ezra. It was more that he enjoyed the lifestyle, and he was a bit of a lone wolf...for a bear. He also had a sense of honor that ran strong. He would never double-cross a friend, which was why he'd earned Trevor's friendship and trust.

Trevor was glad to feel Beth's trembling ease. He rubbed her upper arms with loving strokes, just waiting for her to calm down a little more before he moved them both off the street.

"You feeling any better, honey?" he asked, pulling back slightly to meet her gaze.

"Trevor..." She swallowed hard before continuing. "You were amazing."

Her words surprised him, but they also made him smile.

"You think so?" He dropped a kiss on her lips, uncaring of who saw them. He loved the way she felt in his arms. As if she'd been made to be there.

"I know so. And I want to learn how to fight on land." He was pleased by the steely determination that entered her eyes. This incident hadn't cowed her. It had only made her want to be stronger.

"That's my girl," he whispered. "I'll teach

you anything you want to know, all right?" He couldn't stop smiling, which was a new sensation for him.

"I'll take you up on that," she promised him, her body still and completely under control now that the danger had passed.

Trevor realized a large part of her fright had been in not knowing how to defend herself out of the water. His girl was a warrior, at heart, but she was still learning. It would be his honor—and his pleasure—to teach her self-defense and see her blossom into the tigress she was becoming.

"Will you stay with me up here on land until this is over?" he asked, his heart clenching in anticipation of her answer.

She nodded immediately, setting his heart free. "Nansee sent me. She told me there were sharks making headway through the ward, and the water isn't really safe for me right now."

Trevor frowned. He would've liked her to say she would rather be with him than under the waves, but perhaps it was too soon to hope for that. Still, she was going to stay with him. He'd have time to work on their relationship while she was on land. It would be all right. He could work with that.

"Trev, I think your friend is here. Either that, or we're about to have another incident on Main Street," Brody said, coming up behind Beth. Trevor looked up to see the sheriff's gaze focused behind Trevor, toward where he'd left those three bounty hunters bleeding on the pavement.

Sure enough, there was Ezra, rolling silently into town on his Harley. He'd apparently shut down the engine some distance away and had used the downhill that led into the main part of town to make his approach as close to silent as he could manage. The bike was slowing now as he rolled up to the edge of the battlefield. He met Trevor's gaze and nodded once, parking the bike at the edge of the incident scene.

"Yeah, that's Ezra," Trevor confirmed to Brody. He saw the sheriff give a hand signal to the other bear shifters of his unit, and they let Ezra through without challenge. Trevor noted Ezra took his time to look over the fallen on his way.

"Who's that?" Beth asked, drawing away from Trevor.

He didn't really want to let her go, but there was work to do. He released her with a reassuring squeeze to her shoulder, but he didn't let her go too far. He kept hold of her right hand with his left, unable to relinquish contact completely.

"Honey, that man is a bounty hunter," he told her flat out, noting her little gasp of apprehension. "But I can assure you that you're in no danger from him. He's an old friend of mine, and we've worked together a few times. He's a man of honor, and he's come to help."

"How?" she asked on a whisper.

Trevor smiled as he looked at her. "He's got the inside track on the bounty side of this, and he knows most of the folks working in his field. He also knows all the tricks. Trust me, he's going to be a great help here."

She looked at him for a moment, then seemed to come to a decision. "I trust you, Trevor."

He didn't have time to answer in words because Ezra was almost upon them, but he squeezed her hand. Then, it was time to go to work. Trevor faced Ezra with Beth at his side, determination stiffening his spine. This threat to his mate would not be allowed to continue.

No way. No how.

Beth was amazed by what she'd just witnessed. Not only had Trevor taken on and defeated three huge shifters, but the cavalry—in the form of the town council of Grizzly Cove—had come to help. There had been no hesitation. They'd worked as the tight military unit she'd heard they'd once been to contain the situation and keep her safe.

They'd come to her rescue when there was little in it for them. She knew intellectually that the bears of Grizzly Cove had become allies of her people, but if Jonathan was behind this, there was probably a lot of money to be made by letting her be captured. She hadn't really expected, when push came to shove, that the bears would work this hard to keep her.

It brought a tear to her eye to learn that the bears here were as good as their word. They hadn't let her be taken. They'd put themselves in harm's way to help her.

No one more so than Trevor, of course. She owed him so much, but then again, she loved him. He was her mate.

Wow.

Love. Yeah, that was it. She was in love

with the big bear who had just nearly ripped the arms off three giant guys who had threatened her.

And now, it looked like he'd called in a favor from at least one of his contacts. The man on the motorcycle approached them, and she realized he was as big as Trevor and the other bears of Grizzly Cove. Another bear? One who apparently made his living as a bounty hunter?

Stranger things had happened.

The man stopped a few yards away from them and tilted his head to the side, gesturing behind him, where the town's doctor—a polar bear shifter named Sven—was seeing to some seriously broken bones. The newcomer narrowed his eyes a bit.

"Your work?" he asked, his voice a deceptively lazy drawl.

Trevor nodded. "Know them?"

"Yup," the new man said.

Beth wanted to scream. Did they only speak in single-syllable words?

The new guy's gaze went to their clasped hands. "That her?"

Stars above! What would it take to get a full sentence out of him?

Trevor's hand tightened on hers for a

moment as he seemed to puff out his chest just the tiniest bit. What in the world was going on behind that stoic façade?

"She's mine," was Trevor's surprising reply. The growly tone in which he spoke, as well as the words, simple as they were, sent little shivers of delight down her spine.

The newcomer nodded and looped the mirrored sunglasses he'd been holding in one hand into the neck of his T-shirt. His gaze went from Trevor to her and back again.

"Understood," was his one-word reply.

Beth had to fight a smile. That had been three whole syllables!

CHAPTER ELEVEN

It turned out that Ezra Tate could speak in full sentences, using words of more than one syllable, as Beth found out when Trevor introduced his friend to Big John. They'd moved off the street, leaving the doctor, deputy and a good portion of the town council outside to continue mopping up. The sheriff had already escorted the two men left standing to the jail, which was adjacent to the town hall.

After locking them up in the heretofore unused jail cell and arranging for guards, Sheriff Brody joined Beth, Trevor, Big John and newcomer, Ezra, over in the mayor's office for a quick discussion. Beth remained a silent observer while the men talked tactics, strategy and intel. The focus of the matter was the bounty on her head, which gave her every right to hear what they were talking about, but she readily admitted that their sense of strategy and military operations was way above her pay grade. She was content to let them plan the defense of their town, but since she was the reason for the danger, she was pleased they included her in the meeting.

If it all got too complicated and she believed she was putting too many people in too much danger, she'd just leave. It was her life. They couldn't stop her. She didn't want to, but if it was the only way to protect her friends, she would take her chances on her own.

She had the hope that Trevor might come with her, if she should have to employ that option, but she still wasn't one hundred percent sure. Still, he'd claimed her in front of his friend. He'd come to her defense and made her attackers bleed. The primal part of her nature couldn't help but admire him for that. He was a man strong of character with the deadly skills to back it up. He'd make a good mate to her animal side, as well as her human half...if he was interested.

Although he'd done a lot to prove his desire to keep her safe today, she still wasn't certain if he was on the same page as far as the emotional component went. Did he love her? She just wasn't sure. Hopefully, she'd find the courage to bring up the topic later, when they were alone, but a part of her wanted to be more chicken than predator and simply not ask questions she might not like the answers to.

"So, who do we have in our jail cell?" Brody asked at one point in the men's conversation. Beth stopped woolgathering and refocused on the information being imparted.

"You've got Johnny Balkan. He's the one who pulled the gun. A lynx shifter out of Canada. The one who was a bit smarter and backed off is Wayne Cudkin from Ohio. He's a lone wolf. Usually a good guy, but I hear he's fallen on hard times, which is probably why he took up with the other four. The bounty is big enough to share, even split five ways," Ezra told them, ending with a questioning glance at Beth, as if he was trying to figure out what she'd done to warrant such a price on her head.

"How much are we talking about?" John asked quietly.

"Half a mil. No permanent damage. Delivery by the end of the month." Ezra ticked off the requirements of the bounty as if discussing a shopping list. It made Beth feel a bit queasy to hear herself discussed in such a way, but she knew it wasn't Ezra's fault. This had Jonathan written all over it. "Bounty's been active for a good long while, but nobody knew where she was until about a week ago. That's when the alerts that had been set up started pinging Grizzly Cove, and the insane or desperate began to make plans to invade your territory."

"What happens if she's not turned in by the end of the month?" Brody asked.

Ezra shrugged and sat back in his chair. "Bounty goes away. The thing would have to be reissued at that point, but since there's a strict time limit on this, I get the feeling it won't be. There's something special about the end date." All eyes turned to Beth. Brody's raised eyebrow compelled her to speak.

"I turn twenty-one on the thirty-first," she told them, dread rising as she realized what this must all be about. "My father—my real father—owned a lot of property and it's being held in trust for me until I turn twenty-one. My mother is the legal trustee, but Jonathan—my stepfather—has been using the property, and Mom just signs everything. It could be that he wants to retain control of the real estate."

She was shocked she hadn't thought of this before, but she'd been free for a long time now, and he'd never really sent anyone after her. She'd been safe with the pod. Or so she'd thought.

"How much real estate are we talking about?" John asked.

"I'm not really sure anymore. A lot of it was industrial. Warehouses along the coast. Things like that. Dad had been the leader of my mother's old pod, but it was decimated after his death, and everybody scattered. A lot were killed. Mom never talks about it, but I've heard rumors since running away from home that a school of sharks attacked the pod and killed just about everyone."

"Shapeshifter sharks?" Ezra's voice held suspicion.

Beth nodded. "Probably. I mean, it's the only thing that really makes sense. Mer are usually able to deal with all life in the sea—

even sharks and other predators. We're the apex predator in the ocean…except for the rare shifters we run across, like the occasional family of selkies, dolphins or sharks, but they're even rarer than we are."

"But Jonathan is a shark shifter," Trevor said quietly.

Beth swallowed hard, her suspicions crystallizing. "It's very possible that Jonathan engineered the destruction of my father's pod and took me and my mother so he'd have access to the pod's wealth, which was mostly in my father's name and held in trust for me."

Bright stars! Why hadn't she put this together before? Had she been in that much of a tizzy that she couldn't see what must have been obvious to others? Probably. She'd been doing nothing but surviving, her emotions in tatters, for a very long time.

"And when you turn twenty-one, whatever's left is legally yours," the mayor said.

The sheriff whistled low between his teeth and sat back. "Girl, you've got a massive problem on your hands. Judging by what happened today, that shark bastard isn't going to give you—and your wealth—up without a fight."

"It's not really my money. It belonged to the old pod. If I ever *am* able to claim it, I'll probably relinquish most of it to Nansee for the use of my new pod," she told them, just so they knew she didn't intend to keep it all.

That wasn't the mer way. It would honor her father's memory, and those of his pod who were lost to the sharks, to do the right thing with their wealth.

"We should get Tom to look into the legality behind all of this," John said, naming the town's lawyer. "I also want to look into the attack on your father and his people. It sounds to me, just on the face of it, that Jonathan may have seriously broken shifter laws, for which we might be able to exact punishment." John's gaze went to Trevor.

"If there's a justifiable reason to kill him, it would make this a whole lot easier," Trevor agreed.

Beth was shocked. They talked about killing Jonathan as if it was nothing. Didn't they know he was a shark? He was guarded at all times! They wouldn't be able to get to him, even if it was legal to target him. Were they nuts?

Or...maybe...after what she'd seen on

the street… Maybe there was nobody better equipped to do something like that than the men of Grizzly Cove. Ex-military. All Special Operators. Men who had killed before and would do so again, under the right circumstances. Could this really be one of those times?

The predator that lived in her soul certainly wished it were.

"The end of the month is in just a few days," Trevor said, running through the scenario in his mind. "We just have to keep her safe until then."

He was a little stunned that the woman he'd thought destitute and depending on the charity of her pod was, in fact, an heiress. He had known she'd been hiding things from him, but this was certainly a doozy of a secret.

"She was safe in the water with her pod until they got trapped in the cove by the leviathan," John said, bringing Trevor back to the matter at hand. "But now, even the water isn't quite the safe haven it was. Nansee passed along the reports of sharks trying to cross the ward. They haven't breached it, and according to Urse, they won't be able to if their intent is evil, but she couldn't one-hundred percent guarantee some shark shifter couldn't find a way around the ward—either coming in by land or finding some kind of counter-magic that would allow passage through the water."

"So the safest place is on land, for now, with me," Trevor supplied, reaching for Beth's hand under the conference table.

He'd kept her at his side, but he needed the reassurance of touching her. Thank the Goddess, Beth seemed to understand, her little hand clinging to his.

"We can make the hotel more secure," Brody put in. "I've already got guys patrolling the woods and keeping an eye on the roads leading in and out of town, but it's a lot of area to cover. Concentrating surveillance on the hotel would be a cinch."

"I've already got the room next door set up for Ezra," Trevor told them. "Anyone else who wants to stand guard shifts is more than welcome. Thanks."

"I'll set up a rotation and get the rest of the team in on this," Brody assured him.

"Beth." John's solemn tone underlined the seriousness of his words. "I just want to make sure we're not all leaping to conclusions. I don't think we are, but this needs to be said, just for the record." They weren't actually keeping records, but Trevor understood what Big John was getting at. "Is it true that you don't want to go back to the care and protection of your stepfather, Jonathan?"

Beth gulped and nodded. "That's correct," she said, her voice gaining strength as she went on. "I don't ever want to see him again, if I can help it."

"Hmm. Well, just so you know, that can be arranged. While in the eyes of human law, he's your kin, you should know that under the rules of most shifter communities, he has no claim over you since you're of suitable age and able to make your own decisions about who earns your trust and fealty. If, in the course of our investigations, we discover that he's done even worse than try to coerce you against your will, I might, as Alpha of Grizzly Cove, order the ultimate sanction against him."

Trevor silently hoped they would find a reason to kill the bastard who had terrorized Beth for so long. In fact, he'd like to do the job personally.

"I understand, Alpha," Beth replied.

"And while I would never beg for any sort of leniency for Jonathan, I would ask that if you or your men cross paths with my mother, that you'd do your best not to harm her. She's been hurt enough."

John nodded. "You have my word, Beth. I want you to know that when I extended the invitation to your pod to shelter in the cove, you all became part of our community, and as such, you are all under my protection. I hope you know that you can come to me, or one of my team, any time. We bears take care of our people."

Trevor silently applauded the Alpha's words. Big John was proving to be every bit of the Alpha his men had named him, and Trevor's already good opinion of the man was rising steadily. This was a man who had earned his people's loyalty—with good reason.

Beth seemed moved by John's words, and she choked out a soft *thank you* that was full of emotion. Trevor squeezed her hand in silent support.

He wished he could take all these problems off her shoulders, but it wasn't going to be simple. He would, however, do everything in his power to help her through this rough patch so she could come out on the other side, whole and safe…and hopefully by his side, though he hadn't dared speak to her about mating yet.

He didn't want to scare her off, but the time was coming when his beast half would demand he say something. The bear didn't like uncertainty. He valued action. And he'd push his human half to find out where they stood with the female of their choice. Trevor hoped he could hold off until this situation was resolved, but he had doubts he could make it even a day, much less the few days until the end of the month and Beth's twenty-first birthday.

The town's doctor walked into the room at that point, drawing all eyes. He was a tall Nordic-looking fellow who turned into a giant polar bear on occasion, and like most of the men in John's unit, Trevor had worked with him before. Sven nodded and began his report on the wounded at John's direction.

"According to their IDs, two of the men in my clinic are brothers," Sven reported.

Ezra broke in. "That would be the Gomez brothers. Both are leopard shifters and hail from South America but make their home in Texas now when they're not on the road chasing bounties. I've run across them a few times. Neither one is too bright."

"Trev put them both out of commission for a while. Nasty breaks that even shifter healing would have a hard time with, but I patched them up, and they should recover fully, in time," Sven told them. "The third man is a bit trickier. He had multiple IDs in his wallet, and he's still unconscious. I'll be watching him until he wakes because his brain got knocked around pretty good. I might need to do something about that if he doesn't wake up within the next few hours, but I don't want to get ahead of myself. We're in wait-and-see mode with him for now."

"That would be Shelly Lowenstein," Ezra said. "He likes to use multiple names depending on the job, but he was given the name Sheldon by his parents. He's from Northern California. Another werewolf, affiliated with a lesser Pack near Sacramento. Smarter than the Gomez boys, but still more a brawler than a deep thinker."

"How are you set for security at the clinic, Sven?" John asked.

"I'm fine for now, but I'll need some help

after they start healing. Or we could move the two Gomez brothers to the jail once they start showing signs of recovery. That would leave me with just the one to watch, which I can manage mostly on my own."

"Good. Coordinate with Brody on that. He's distributing manpower and working on a roster," John told the doctor. "In the meantime, we need to be getting the word out to the rest of the residents to lay low, stick close to home, and report anything out of the ordinary at once. I've got a few calls to make, and I need to coordinate with Nansee and make sure she knows what we're doing on land. Trevor, you're in charge of Beth. Is that okay with you?" John asked Beth, almost as an afterthought. Trevor was relieved when she agreed without argument.

Brody's cell phone beeped, interrupting the meeting, and he stood to take the call. It wasn't a long talk, and when he came back into the office, his face was grim.

"That was Jack. A group of shark shifters just tried to enter the water from the beach near his house. He and his nearest neighbors went bear on their asses and stopped most of them, he thinks, but he can't guarantee they got all of them. Grace dove in to warn the mer, and Jack's going a little nuts over it." Brody swore, but there was understanding on the sheriff's face. Jack was mated to Grace. If she was in danger, no wonder he was losing his shit.

"Any casualties on our side?" John asked. "Do they need Sven to come out?"

"No. All present and accounted for," Brody reported. "Not too much damage to our guys. Jack said it was pretty obvious the other side wasn't so good on land, but they had a lot of firepower on them that had to be neutralized."

It made sense to Trevor that shark shifters would be killers in the water, but judging by Beth's lack of skill on land, the sharks probably relied on weapons when in their human form. They probably hadn't bargained on encountering bear shifters—or if they had considered it, they probably thought they could shoot their way out of a confrontation.

That had been a big miscalculation on their part. Probably a fatal one.

"Were there any survivors?" John asked in a neutral tone.

"Not a lot," Brody answered in the same tone. "According to Jack, the sharks were rather insistent on a shooting war but had problems when our guys took it in close. In the course of disarming the bad guys, our boys might've used a bit of zeal."

John merely nodded. "Understood. Do we have anybody we can send out to help with mop up, XO?"

Ah, there it was, Trevor thought. Evidence that the military unit had never really retired. The Alpha had just called his second-in-command by the military abbreviation of XO, which stood for executive officer. No matter that they might be wearing civilian clothes now and playing civilian roles of mayor and sheriff, they were still commanding officer and XO.

"I'll arrange it, sir," Brody replied.

Yeah, the bears were just fooling themselves if they thought they were done with the military lifestyle. The minute danger threatened, they fell back into the pattern too easily.

Which was a good thing. They were living in dangerous times. It was good to have a group of kick-ass guys around you that you could count on. That's why Trevor was part of with Moore's group, and that's what the bears of Grizzly Cove had going on here.

"All right," John said, returning to the discussion at large with a grim expression. "You two hunker down at the hotel. Take the bounty hunter with you." John nodded toward Ezra. "We'll arrange a protection detail starting immediately. If these bastards dare to come into our territory and stir shit up, they'll get what they deserve."

Trevor found himself joining a chorus of strong *yes, sir* that sounded around the room. Even Ezra joined in, and Trevor remembered the other man had been in Force Recon when he'd been a Marine. Once a guy spent time in Spec Ops, he always carried that special mojo around with him. That, and the discipline.

The Grizzly Cove bears hadn't been out of the service all that long, so the soldier mentality was a bit closer to the surface. Trevor had never really left the service, transitioning from active duty with Uncle Sam's forces to mercenary work without much of a break in between. Discipline was still a way of life for him, but Ezra had faded into the civilian sphere, fitting in a bit better than the others in the room. He might look like some sort of bad-boy biker, but Trevor knew he had it where it counted, and he was glad to have his help in keeping Beth safe.

The meeting broke up shortly after John's final orders, and Beth was escorted to the hotel by a small platoon of bear shifters. A perimeter guard was already in place, and the hotel itself had been searched and secured well before their arrival. The other rooms would remain in lockdown until this matter was settled.

When they were finally alone in Trevor's room, he didn't waste time on words, he just drew Beth into his arms and held her tight for long minutes. She snuggled into him. Her trembling had disappeared from the aftermath of the battle, but he knew she was close to overwhelmed by all that had happened in such a short period of time.

He was used to quick change in his line of work, but he knew it was harder for civilians to deal with the upheavals of conflict. Beth wrapped her arms around him and squeezed tight, her eyes shut as her cheek rested against his chest. The moment was filled with silent communication, emotion rich between them. Her hold on him spoke of trust and gratitude, care and appreciation.

"Did I say thank you?" Beth whispered.

"No need," Trevor replied.

She would never have to thank him for keeping her safe. It was his honor and his pleasure. But she didn't really know that yet. He had to figure out a way to get her to agree that they were mates without coming on too strong and scaring her off.

She pushed back, both hands on his chest, so she could meet his gaze. "You were amazing, Trevor. You seem all calm and cool on the outside, but inside is this wild man who probably knows more ways to down an opponent than I could ever count."

Trevor pretended to consider. "Mm. Eight hundred and forty-two."

"What?"

"That was the last count I had, but I stopped keeping track when I was about eighteen. Sorry."

He liked the way she caught on to his joke, laughing with him. It felt good to share a moment of joy after the turmoil of the earlier part of the day.

"You think we'll be safe here?" she asked after the laughter died down. He hated the fear in her eyes.

"Better here tonight than anywhere else. Ez is next door, and half of a retired-in-name-only Delta Force unit is patrolling the dark. Nothing's going to get past them." Trevor had had his suspicions about the team of ex-military bears who called this place home before he'd arrived, but after seeing them in action, he was glad to have them nearby.

"If you trust the set up, then I won't second-guess you. It's your business to know, right?" she said reasonably, but he knew deep down she couldn't help the fear. He wrapped his arms around her once more, rocking her gently from side to side.

"Nothing and no one is going to get to you. I promise." And Trevor never made promises lightly. When he did, he meant it.

A discreet knock on the door made him let her go. The knock was followed by a gruff voice. "It's me, Zak. I brought you guys some dinner."

Trevor relaxed a bit, motioning for Beth to stand out of the line of sight of the door as he went to answer it. He opened the door cautiously, but it really was only Zak, and Ezra was watching from the door of his own room, one door down. He gave Trevor the all-clear signal as Zak handed over a large paper shopping bag that smelled wonderful.

"I figured you two would need some

sustenance. There's also a box from the bakery for dessert." He handed over a second bag, this one made of plastic. "And here's a selection of soft drinks, bottled water and other stuff you could probably use."

"Sorry I don't have a tip for you," Trevor joked with Grizzly Cove's resident Cajun chef. "But I won't say no to room service. Thanks, Zak."

"My pleasure. Tell Beth I hope she likes the salmon. There's also gumbo and shrimp Creole. I tried to cook a few different fish dishes for her, but there are also some hamburgers in there if that's what you're in the mood for."

"Sounds like you cooked for an army," Trevor commented, impressed by the weight of the large shopping bag.

"Just planning ahead. You two might get hungry later, and I know there's a fridge and microwave in your room. Although I wouldn't normally recommend nuking any of my food, it'll do in a pinch." Zak winked as he turned to leave.

"Thanks again, Zak. I owe you," Trevor called after him.

Trevor watched the hallway until Zak was

gone, then shifted his focus to Ezra. "Did you get supplies?"

The bounty hunter nodded. "I've got enough to tide me over. Deputy Zak delivered the first care package to me before knocking on your door."

Trevor smiled at his friend's curious look. "Oh, you're in for a treat. Zak owns a restaurant, and his specialty is gourmet Cajun."

Ezra's eyebrows rose, and he looked into his room with a bit of eagerness.

Trevor didn't have to say much more. He shut the door, letting Ezra watch to be sure it was secure before the bounty hunter returned to his room...and his unexpected treat of a dinner.

He and Beth ate dinner together, talking a bit about the situation in which she found herself. She told Trevor more about her stepfather's business enterprises. She didn't know many details, but she'd been observant enough while living in his house to glean a few facts. The picture wasn't a pretty one.

"When you get control of your inheritance, you're going to have to do something about Jonathan's activities," Trevor told her, knowing the task would be difficult and most likely dangerous, as well.

"I know." Beth pushed away from the small table, having finished eating, and began to clean up. "I'm not looking forward to it, but it's important. I talked to Nansee about it in a roundabout way. I couldn't tell her all the details, but I sounded her out on some of it. Mer have contacts in places you wouldn't necessarily expect."

"Did she give you any advice?" Trevor was curious about those contacts Beth hinted at. Intel was his specialty, and it sounded like the mer leader might be a good source to cultivate.

"Some," Beth replied, bringing the small wastebasket over to the side of the table and brushing crumbs into it. "It was hard to get solid steps to take when I couldn't tell her all the details, but she promised to help when I was ready to tell her everything. I think she can dismantle some of the things that are based along the coast, and she might even be able to call in some favors to stop illegal shipments that are already on their way overseas."

"That's good. But you might have to get more hands-on with some of the things Jonathan has in play. If you own the properties, you may need to start legal proceedings to evict or shut down some of the businesses operating out of them. The lawyers here in Grizzly Cove might be able to help with that. And I want you to know, I'm ready, willing and able to help if you need me. I'd be happy to help in whatever way I can." He wanted to say so much more, but he wasn't sure this was the right time.

Beth put the wastebasket back in the corner and came over to sit on his lap. She'd taken him by surprise, but he was more than willing to make room for her in his embrace. He loved having her close to him.

"I might just take you up on that offer, my friend. But for now, I think I'd just like to forget my troubles for a little while. Can you help me with that?" She blinked innocently at him, and just like that, he grew hard.

He knew she could feel it against her bottom because she wiggled a bit and smiled at him. The minx. She knew what she was doing to him. But he wasn't complaining. He liked this playful side of her too much to put an end to it.

Instead, he stood with her wrapped in his arms and carried her to the bed. Luckily, this hotel was built with bear shifters in mind and the beds were large enough for them both. Trevor placed her down on the bedspread and took great pleasure in kissing every inch of skin as he undressed her.

When she was naked and spread out before him, he stood back to just look at her while he divested himself of his own clothing. She watched, and he liked the half-lidded looks she gave him as he peeled off his shirt. Thankfully, he'd had time to clean up a bit from the fight earlier in the day, though he hadn't been injured. Still, he'd earned a few bruises that were already healing—mostly on his knuckles.

When he was naked, he went back to the bed, putting one knee on the mattress. Beth surprised him by sitting up and grabbing his hand. She ran her fingertips lightly over his bruised knuckles, then brought them to her lips for a sweet kiss.

"I'm sorry you got hurt defending me, but I'll never forget how brave you were, Trevor," she whispered. The look in her eyes made his heart go pitter-pat, but he didn't know what to say.

He knew what to do, though. He joined her on the bed and kissed her deeply, pouring all the things he couldn't say into the kiss.

CHAPTER TWELVE

Trevor's kiss was so full of emotion. She wondered if he realized what he was doing to her. He was making her fall in love with him even more—if such a thing was possible. She'd thought she'd known enough about him yesterday to say that they were mates, but she had learned today that there were facets to this man that made him ever more appealing.

The Goddess certainly knew what She was doing when She put certain people together. Beth sent a little prayer of thanks heavenward as she rolled with Trevor, landing on top of him on the big bed. Just where she wanted to be.

There wasn't time, or need, for much preliminary. She'd been wet for him since the moment she saw him walk, unscathed, past the bodies of the men who had threatened her. The predator in her soul had grown to respect him in that moment, recognizing its equal. In fact, her beast half figured there was quite a bit Trevor could teach her about hunting and killing…which was just part of the animal that shared her soul.

It didn't really understand the softer emotions, but it respected strength, and their mate was among the strongest men she'd ever seen. Even better, he had used his strength and skill to protect her, not to cage her. For that alone, he had earned her inner beast's loyalty.

She took him in her hand, reaching between their bodies to do so. He was hard and long, thick and warm. And she wanted him. She wanted him now.

Rubbing against him, she positioned herself over him and pressed down, taking him more easily this time, as if her body had made itself into the perfect place for his. She moaned when he filled her, already close to the edge. It didn't take much when they were together.

She began to move, but it wasn't controlled by any stretch of the imagination. She growled in frustration as her desire overrode her coordination. Finally, Trevor took control, rolling them until they were on their sides, facing each other. He lifted her top leg over his hip, tugging under her knee so that she was wrapped around him, the pressure oh-so-delicious where their bodies were still joined.

The friction made shivers of delight race up and down her spine. She wasn't going to last long. The day had been too emotional. Too fraught with dangerous highs and lows. The only thing that was clear in the muddle of her life was this. This joining of skin to skin, body to body, Beth to Trevor and back again. This was something she could understand and enjoy without thinking too hard.

The odd angle made for delicious sensations within her, and when she opened her eyes, Trevor was there, looking at her. His languid gaze met hers, the moment intimate and unique in her experience. Never before had she felt so close to a man—not just physically but emotionally, as well.

He was her mate, but she didn't know how to tell him. Still, by the look in his eyes, she wondered if he didn't already realize the truth. Did he not know how to broach the subject either? Wouldn't that be funny if they were both hesitant to bring up the topic that could unite them forever?

Trevor shifted slightly, making her gasp. The change brought him in contact with her clit, and then, all thought ceased as her body took over. The sensations he invoked rode through her bloodstream, up her spine and out to every sensitive nerve ending. Waves of pleasure hit her in time with his increasing thrusts until she was swept under the final tidal wave of pleasure.

She cried out his name, grasping at his shoulders as she came, feeling him come with her, going rigid in her arms and in her body. Warmth filled her. Physical warmth and the emotional warmth of being closer to the man she loved at this moment than she had ever been to anyone else.

She cherished the minutes that followed where Trevor held her, petting her, stroking her skin and whispering gentle endearments as they both came down from the highest high yet. They were both still new to each other. She wondered what sex would be like with him after they'd been together for a while and speculated that she might not survive such pleasure. Then again, it would be an amazing experience, even if it did ruin her for any other man.

Who was she kidding? She was ruined for anyone else already. Her heart, her mer half, her human half and her soul were set on Trevor. Anyone else could never compete. He was her match in every way, and she would never tire of his lovemaking or simply being with him, no matter what they were doing.

She dozed in his arms, a smile on her lips.

A few hours later, in the deepest part of the night, Trevor's cell phone pinged. He woke instantly, having trained himself to sleep light over many years on combat duty. He grabbed for the phone that was set to a special low-level red illumination he'd programmed so as not to ruin his night vision. He took one look at the screen and sat upright in the bed, waking Beth. She didn't sleep nearly as lightly as he, but he could see her struggling to come to full alert.

"Ezra messaged. There's activity behind the hotel," he told her, summing up the message that had been in code, but relayed a lot more details that would only worry her at the moment.

"Fighting?" she asked, frowning as she reached for her clothing. She left the underwear and went right for shirt and pants, saving time. Trevor did the same, only he added a few weapons to his ensemble. In fact, that reminded him...

He opened the only closet in the room and...yes, there it was. He'd asked John to get one of the mer to drop this off, and he was glad they'd been able to do it.

"Your trident," he said, taking the long, lethally sharp weapon out of the closet and handing it to her. "I figured it might make you feel safer if you had a weapon you were familiar with."

She took the trident in one hand and threw the other arm around his neck, drawing him down for a quick kiss. There were tears in her eyes when she pulled back.

"Thank you," she whispered. "It does help, even if I'm not that graceful on land."

"Yet," he added, holding her gaze. He'd teach her how to defend herself on land as

221

soon as they had a moment to breathe. He didn't like seeing her so vulnerable and scared. He cupped the side of her head and kissed her. "It'll be okay. I promise," he whispered, meaning every word. "And you look like a total badass with that trident." He gave her a smile, glad to see an answering upturn of her lips as he drew away. "When we get back, I want you to pose for me with it…and nothing else."

"We're going out there?" she asked, neatly bypassing his request, but he guessed he shouldn't have been surprised, what with the tense situation and all.

"They're going to need my help," Trevor replied. "And I think this is probably something you need to see. Much as I'd like to hide you away from the action and keep you safe from all harm, wrapping you in a cocoon and not letting you take an active part in your own defense isn't what I want. You need to witness the take down of your stepfather's men. You need to be present so you can fully understand that they'll never get to you. No way. No how. Not while I draw breath. And not while the bears of Grizzly Cove have claimed you as one of their own. They protect their people, and it's important to you, and all the mer in the cove, that you see that in action."

He could have gone on about how the mer and the bears might be on the verge of forming a unique society here, in the test waters of the cove, but judging by the noises coming from outside the hotel, he didn't have time. Even through the mostly sound-proofed walls, he could hear the clash of battle. Ezra had imparted numbers in his text, and the bears were definitely fewer than the attackers, but they could handle whatever came—with Trevor's help. They might be outnumbered, but they'd never be outclassed.

For one thing, they were defending their own territory. Nothing spiked a shifter's ire like a threat to his home. That the thugs Beth's stepfather employed either didn't realize this or didn't seem to care would work against them. Big time.

But Trevor still needed to be out there, to make up numbers and end this faster. The shorter the battle, the better for all concerned. Already, he could hear Ezra outside, fighting alongside the Grizzly Cove bears, his roar distinctive and familiar. Trevor needed to help, but he also needed to be sure Beth could not only see what was going on, but be as safe as possible while she observed just what the bears could do.

He'd thought about this long and hard before realizing she had to be part of her own rescue. Her stepfather had nearly broken her spirit, and this was an important step in restoring it. If he hid her from the reality of the fight, she might never recover from the fear her stepfather had instilled in her for so very long. Trevor didn't want that for her. Beth should be fearless—like the other mer he'd met.

She was a huntress in the ocean. She'd already overcome her past to that extent. Now, he needed to help her find her footing on land.

It might be dangerous, but he was confident in his ability to keep her safe. He'd also done a little preemptive work, suspecting this sort of thing might happen. If all went as planned, Beth wouldn't be left all alone while he engaged the enemy. In fact, she'd be part of a group that would protect her with their very lives, should it become necessary, while still allowing her to feel as if she was part of her own defense.

"Come on, honey," he told her now. "We

have work to do."

Hefting her trident in one hand, Beth was beside him as they approached the door. Trevor motioned her to the side, and he opened the door, going out first to face possible danger head on. Once he was sure the hallway was secure, he called to her to join him. First hurdle crossed. Now for the door that led to the outside. It was a thick glass affair, through which he could already see the battle.

As he stepped closer, he saw three smaller figures emerge from the room closest to the door. Beth gasped, but this was according to Trevor's plan. The three women came closer, each holding a wicked-looking trident in one hand and sporting several other sheathed blades Trevor could see.

"My old hunting party," Beth whispered. "Sirena, Jetty, and Grace," she named them as they came forward. Trevor was humbled to see that Beth was moved near to tears.

"Your man Trevor there let us know what might happen," Sirena, the leader of their old hunting party said as she stood next to Beth. "We agreed to be ready to stand with you."

"Beth, you don't have to face this alone.

We're your sisters," Grace said, touching Beth's arm.

Trevor suspected the others would have said more, but time was of the essence. He began moving toward the door once again, and they followed. They weren't exactly a military unit, but they had trained together to hunt in the ocean, protecting and providing for the pod. They were warriors, though their skills in the water were probably much sharper than on land. Still, they had those long, pointy tridents, and they gave every appearance of knowing how to use them.

And they loved Beth like a sister. That counted for a lot. They would stand by her while the bears dealt with the thugs, and should anything even come close to threatening her, they would stand with her against all comers.

These ladies were mated to bears now, and those bears would be watching over the hunting party too, Trevor knew. It was the only way he could get agreement for the women to participate, but the other men knew their mates, and they'd admitted the women would not be happy with them if they didn't let them help defend their friend. Those bears had known what they were in for when they mated with warrior mermaids. Trevor wanted Beth to have the same fierce spirit, and this was a significant part of cultivating it, dangerous as it might be.

There were no lights on in the hall. Trevor had done that deliberately so anyone looking in through that thick glass door wouldn't be able to see much, even with sharp shifter eyesight. He paused before that final barrier to the melee taking place just a few yards distant.

"You have a defensible location picked out?" Trevor asked Sirena, the leader of the hunting party.

She nodded confidently. "We've got the high ground."

Intimately familiar with the layout of the hotel, Trevor knew there was a service stairway only a few feet from the door that could give them quick access to the roof. It was a good spot.

"Marla and Janice are already up there, keeping the area secure," Jetty added, giving Trevor a nod.

Maybe they weren't a military unit, but they were warriors nonetheless. Trevor approved of their precautions.

"All right. I'll cover your ascent," he told

them.

He was certain the bear mates of these women would all be keeping one eye on the stairway. It was the only way on or off the roof, barring climbing gear. No one would be allowed to infiltrate close to that staircase. Absolutely no one.

"Ready?" He was all business now, about to enter the battle. The women seemed the same, which impressed the hell out of Trevor. He hadn't fought alongside many females in his time, but if these gals were any indication, that was his loss.

"On three," Sirena told him, joining him in the countdown before he opened the door, and they all sprang into action.

When they hit one, Trevor opened the door, and they burst into the night. The women turned for the stairway while Trevor kept watch, taking stock of the action at the same time.

He heard a gasp as Beth grabbed his arm. He looked at her, noting her skin had gone pale, and she was staring at one section of the fighting in particular.

A group of three men were standing off to one side, just watching. The two flanking the central man engaged occasionally, as if they were protecting the man in the middle. Trevor's eyes narrowed.

"That's Jonathan," Beth whispered, clearly stunned by seeing her stepfather had come after her in person.

Trevor turned his back to the battle—perhaps foolishly, but it was more important to him at the moment to block any view of Beth. He put himself between her smaller body and the watchers. He'd noticed that Jonathan seemed to be looking for something...or someone. No doubt, he'd just been waiting for Beth to make an appearance, and Trevor wasn't about to let her stand out in the open and let the bastard get a good look.

"To the staircase. Now," he barked as quietly as he could. The other three women were close, but had moved more toward the safety of the enclosed staircase. If he could just get Beth behind the siding-covered rail, Jonathan wouldn't see her. "Crouch as you go up and hide behind the siding. Don't let him see you," Trevor said urgently. Thankfully, Beth's legs began moving as he gave her instructions. She was no longer frozen in place by shock.

He continued to block as she moved

quickly toward the stairs, but he didn't breathe easy until she was on the first steps, surrounded by her friends. Only then, when she was about halfway up the stairs, did he turn back to see what was going on with the battle. Thankfully, Jonathan hadn't moved. He hadn't seen her.

Or had he?

Trevor got an itchy feeling between his shoulder blades. Unable to ignore it, he started up the stairs. The women were already near the top, but he moved fast, following them. He had to see for himself that the roof was secure. He wouldn't be happy until he'd checked every corner.

Something was off. He didn't know what, but there was something that made his skin crawl.

Trevor flowed onto the roof behind the women. "Watch the stairs," was his only comment as he passed Sirena, heading for the three-foot high façade that ringed the entire roof. He'd inspect every inch of it.

Trevor was aware of Beth following a few feet behind him, her trusty trident in her hand. He wished she'd stay closer to the others, but he couldn't really justify telling her to go away. For one thing, that would be mean and he never wanted to hurt her feelings. For another, she might be safer closer to him. His pride made him think that he could defend her better than anyone else—especially a group of women he'd never seen in action. He had no idea if their fighting skills were any good at all. Sure, they looked fierce, but what if he trusted them to take care of Beth and they failed? What then?

He was about two thirds of the way around the roof line when he saw it. Grapples. More than one. Dark, to blend in with the dark roofing materials, which was why he hadn't seen them from a distance. And there was movement. Someone was climbing.

"Get back!" he ordered in a rasp. "They're coming over the roof. Go back to the stairs and hold the escape route."

He didn't have time to say more because the enemy was upon him. Three men in black fatigues bounded over the knee wall, heading straight for him. He saw the gleam of a pistol aimed toward the women, and he dove for it, knocking the gun out of the man's hand as they both crashed to the ground.

He kicked upward to break the hand of a second man, who also held a gun, but he couldn't prevent a shot being fired. It went wild though, knocked off course by Trevor's destruction of the man's wrist.

As if that single shot was some kind of signal that they no longer had to be quiet, other guns started firing below. All hell was breaking loose down there, and the bears of Grizzly Cove probably had their hands full. If these three were going to be stopped, it was up to Trevor.

He disarmed the third man, sending the handgun sailing over the edge of the roof, but all three were still standing, now sporting sharp hunting knives. Great. And as long as those grapples were still there, other climbers could join them at any minute.

He spared a glance to the wall and noticed Jetty standing near the grapples, a sharp blade in her hand as she cut the lines that led down to the ground. Unless the guys down there had more grapples, no more would be coming up that way.

Trevor almost smiled as he set to work on the three men. He hadn't expected a knife fight when he'd gotten up this morning, but he was game. He'd already broken the dominant wrist of one opponent, so that guy wasn't doing much except harassing Trevor, trying to make openings for his friends to advance. It wasn't working, but Trevor gave them an A for effort. At least they were working as a team, which was more than he'd expected.

It made them a little harder to defeat, but Trevor was confident. It took about ten minutes longer than it should have, but eventually, all three of the attackers were down and out of the action. One was dead, or close to it. The other two unconscious. Good enough, Trevor thought, turning to check on the women.

He'd kept an eye on them as much as he could, and they were all still okay, holding their tridents like they meant business as they guarded the staircase. Trevor jogged over to check the descent, then turned back to the women. They had a right to input on this, since it was their safety at stake.

"Do you want to stay up here or go below? You could hole up in a room in the hotel, or make for water. It's your call since you know your strengths better than I do." It would kill him to let Beth go if they chose water, but if it was the only way to keep her safe, then he'd do what he had to do.

Trevor had turned his back on the staircase for the quick moment it took to talk to the ladies. They were facing him, but it was Beth who alerted him to what was probably the stupidest move he'd ever made. She shouted his name, at the same time, raising her trident like a javelin.

He realized in the nick of time that he should probably duck, and he hit the deck as that ultra-sharp three-pronged spear sailed through the air where he'd just been standing. He turned his head, and, as if in slow motion, he saw the trident hit Jonathan squarely in the chest.

The crime boss's face held a look of abject surprise for the moment it took him to realize he was already dead. Red bloomed as other tridents hit him in other parts of his body. The mermaids were backing up their sister, making sure the threat was dead, once and for all.

Jonathan stumbled back, falling down the stairway, taking out his goons as he fell. They all ended up in a pile at the foot of the stairs, Jonathan's dying body topmost...but not for long.

One by one, the hired killers worked their

way out from under their dead boss. Most immediately put their hands up in the universal sign of surrender. A few kept fighting out in the open space behind the hotel until a piercing whistle cut through the night.

"Your boss is dead," Ezra said bluntly, once he had everyone's attention. "If you keep fighting, you will be too. Get it?"

Beth shouted from the rooftop as Trevor held her back from exposing herself to possible gunfire.

"And there's nobody left who will pay your fees. Jonathan used my money, but no more. Consider yourselves fired."

"She can't do that," one bleeding miscreant yelled. "We have contracts!"

"Come on, Fred," Ezra said to a man on the edge of the crowd. "I know you and the Beaslys, and Ripcord and Whit are all bounty hunters, same as me. The man who put up the bounty for the girl is lying dead at the bottom of the stairs. Ain't nobody gonna pay for her now."

A few curses sounded from the periphery of the crowd of fighters as weapons were thrown down and men knelt in the sand, their fingers interlaced as they put their hands on top of their heads. At least those guys knew how to surrender.

"As for any of you with contracts," Beth made the word sound like a curse, "I'm in charge now. I'll review your supposed contracts with my lawyer, and we'll come to some agreement, but if you really feel you still are under contract to SeaLife Enterprises," she named the shell company under which Jonathan had done all his business—dirty and otherwise, "then as the new CEO, I'm ordering you to stand down and surrender to these bears, whose territory you just invaded without provocation."

Hot damn. Trevor was proud of his mate. This had worked out better than he'd hoped. Not only had she taken down her nemesis, but she'd found her nerve and stepped up to put an end to the bloodshed. Like a boss.

"All right," one of the thugs who'd been guarding Jonathan said with a sigh. "You heard the lady. If we ever want to get paid, we'd better listen to her. I know for a fact that the reason J wanted her so bad is that she's the one who inherited all that money and property. If he didn't control her, he didn't control the wealth, and now that he's gone, it's all hers to do with as she pleases."

The thug with more-than-average brains for his line of work looked directly at Beth. "I assume you're pulling the plug?"

"You've got that right," she affirmed in a strong voice that made Trevor proud.

More groans from the rest of the men, but they began to follow the bounty hunters' example and knelt on the ground, linking their hands together on top of their heads. Trevor could hardly believe it. The Grizzly Cove jail was going to be overflowing tonight, but it looked like the hostilities were over. Thank the Goddess.

CHAPTER THIRTEEN

Dawn was just breaking over the distant hills when the final enemy surrendered. The entire town of Grizzly Cove came out to help with the cleanup. Beth's hunting party retrieved their tridents from Jonathan's body, going down to the shore to wash the blood from their weapons in a ceremony that was as old as the hunting parties themselves.

Sirena, as leader of the hunting party that had been officially disbanded when they moved to Grizzly Cove but was still alive in their hearts, spoke the ancient words to Poseidon, Lord of the Deep, and the

Goddess, Ruler of the Tides. She spoke for the souls of the lost—even Jonathan's—and prayed for peace and the strength to maintain it.

Beth was aware of Trevor keeping track of her movements from a distance, but it didn't bother her. In fact, she found it kind of sweet. And she valued the fact that he didn't make any demands that she stay with him or tell him what she was up to with her friends. He let her be her own person, which was something her stepfather had never allowed.

When they were done cleansing their spirits and their weapons, Beth hugged each member of her old hunting party and thanked them for coming to her aid. Each one dismissed her profuse thanks with the simple statement that they were family and that's what sisters did for each other. Beth was deeply touched.

When the three mated women moved off into the arms of their mates, Beth knew it was time to talk to Trevor. There was a lot of work ahead of her if she was going to unravel Jonathan's criminal enterprises. She'd have to make a start, and she figured Trevor was just the man to help her figure out where and how.

Nansee and some of the mer arrived to help, as well, and Marla and Janice, as the only two who were still unmated from Beth's old hunting party, went to fill in the pod leader on events. More than a few of Jonathan's henchmen had been water shifters. Sharks mostly, Beth thought. They would have to face the law of the sea, and Nansee would be the one to mete out punishment to the survivors.

Trevor came over to Beth, and she went into his arms, glad of his warmth after the tumult of the pre-dawn. They stood quietly for a few moments, gazing out at the cove as the sun kissed the water. Behind them, the task of dealing with the injured and dead went on, the inhabitants of Grizzly Cove rallying to help.

"Brody's got his hands full at the sheriff's office," Trevor told her. "Ezra's helping him sort the bounty hunters from the henchmen, and Big John is laying down the law. He'll probably let the majority of the bounty hunters go with a warning never to set foot in his territory again on pain of death. The goons who are mobile will have to be assessed on a case-by-case basis, but the majority of the ones who survived are in the clinic. Drew's mother, who is a priestess, is saying prayers over the dead."

Beth let that statement ring in the air for a moment as she realized how bad things had been just a few hours before. She stood facing the water, Trevor's arms around her shoulders as she leaned into his side. He made her feel safe, but he also made her feel strong. He was such a good man. A mate any woman could be proud of.

"Is it really over?" she asked, still a bit shell shocked after the events of the night.

By way of answer, Trevor held his free hand out in front of them. In it was a sleek, top of the line cell phone.

"This is Jonathan's phone. You'll probably need this, and the numbers it contains, to begin to unravel his criminal empire." He handed it to her with no hesitation.

Beth took it, but kept her hand over his as she turned her head to meet his gaze. "I'll need help," she told him quietly, hoping he would volunteer.

Trevor didn't disappoint. "I'll make sure you have whatever you need, honey." He sealed his words with a gentle kiss as the sun rose fully from behind the eastern hills, the first rays bathing them in golden light as they stood on the rocky shore of the cove.

The first call Beth made was to her mother. It was an awkward conversation that led to her mother breaking down in tears when she learned Jonathan was dead. At first, Beth wasn't sure if her mother was crying due to grief at her husband's passing, but it soon became apparent that her mother's tears were ones of abject relief.

"Do you want to come up here, to Grizzly Cove?" Beth asked her mother. "I think my new pod would welcome you."

Beth took strength from knowing Trevor was only a few feet away, there to support her through this difficult conversation. She didn't mind that he could hear everything. After today, she really had no secrets left that she wanted to hide from him. Her mother countered Beth's offer, by asking if Beth would come back to Catalina Island, but that was a non-starter.

"No, Mama. I'm never going back to Jonathan's house. Never. I'd rather burn it down than ever set foot in it again. For now, I'm staying here. I'm sorry." Beth was firm, but adamant. She would never go back to that gilded prison. Never.

Her mother was so glad to be free of the tyrant that had threatened Beth's life to keep her mother in line that she was sobbing on the other end of the phone again. Beth hadn't realized Jonathan was using her as a pawn against her mother. It made a lot of sense though.

A lot of other things Beth hadn't really understood began to make sense as she rifled through the contacts list and text messages on Jonathan's phone. His email accounts were another eye opener, and she spent a good few hours using a printer borrowed from town hall, creating a documented paper trail she could follow if need be.

Trevor had suggested printing out the emails, just in case Jonathan had an ally who could make all the evidence disappear. Right now, she had access, but once word of his death got around, the evidence might dry up unexpectedly.

Trevor was a huge help in identifying the most important information. Beth learned a lot about why he was considered an intelligence expert over the hours of that morning. He'd helped set her up in a spare hotel room that was unfurnished. He'd brought in a desk and the borrowed printer, a few reams of paper, file folders, pens, pencils, highlighters… All the things she'd need to get to work. Then, he'd brought her snacks and drinks to tide her over while she worked.

He helped for the first couple of hours, but when she finally got the hang of following the intricate trails Trevor showed her how to find, he left her with Grace and Jack, who had come to offer their help. Jack, she knew, was meant to act as a guard, while Grace and she did the paperwork. It was a good arrangement and left her with friendly company that Trevor was certain would look after her safety.

She liked that he cared enough to arrange such things. And she was grateful to find that Grace was still her friend even though she'd mated one of the bears and left the water, for the most part. They had a good time while they discovered deal after rotten deal that Jonathan had been part of. Beth was certain of one thing after hours of weeding through the filth that was Jonathan's email trail—heads were gonna roll.

She wouldn't let this evil empire stand any longer than she had to. The work of dismantling it had already begun with a few well-placed email messages. More would follow. As would a long consultation with the best lawyers in Grizzly Cove, a mated pair that were both very experienced. For the first time in her life, Beth felt confident about her future.

In every area, except one.

For all his care of her, she still wasn't completely sure about Trevor. Did he want to be her mate? Or was he merely interested for now, but not forever? It was killing her, not knowing where she stood, but there was a lot going on right now. She'd have to wait to get him alone…and work up the courage…to ask him what could be the most important question of her life.

Trevor took a few minutes that afternoon to request a meeting with the Grizzly Cove Alpha. He needed to set a few things in motion—or at least see if any of his tentative plans had a chance in hell of coming to fruition. Finding his mate had been a blessing, but he'd need to juggle a few very important things to make it all work out. He

went into John's office, ready to lay it all on the line. This meeting would make or break the best plan he'd been able to come up with. He had to get it right.

Both John and his right-hand man, Brody, were in the office. Trevor had talked to John a bit about his plans, but he didn't know if the Alpha bear had told his second about it. Of course, if things worked out, everyone would know sooner rather than later, so it really didn't matter.

"Thanks for seeing me," Trevor said politely, taking the seat in John's office right in front of the big desk. Brody was to his side, in the other guest chair.

"No problem at all. What's on your mind, son?" John asked, his full attention on Trevor now that he was in the office.

"Thing is, sir," Trevor figured straight out was better than beating around the bush, "I'd like to discuss that strategy we were talking about a while ago."

"Good," John replied while Brody sent Trevor a questioning look.

"Something going on?" Brody challenged, seeming annoyed to be left out of the loop.

Trevor came clean. "Beth is my mate," he stated in a strong tone that brooked no argument.

Brody seemed to relax, smiling as he relaxed back in his chair. "Yeah, we kinda figured."

"We?" Trevor asked the sheriff.

"All of us saw you claim her on the street when Ezra asked who she was. By now, we've learned to recognize the less obvious signs too," Brody told him. "We all figured you were a goner."

"Happily, a lot of my men have found their mates since settling here." There was satisfaction in the Alpha's voice. Papa bear was happy with his growing family.

But would he be as happy to add another bear to the fold? That's what Trevor had come to find out.

"Thing is, I can't really ask Beth to move to Wyoming. There's not a lot of water on our mountain suitable for a mermaid. In fact, most of the water we do have is frozen a large part of the year." Trevor tried to joke, but inside, he was nervous as hell.

A lot was riding on this man's response to Trevor's request. They'd already talked a bit about ways Trevor's skills could mesh with the team already living in Grizzly Cove, but they hadn't talked about this kind of personal stuff in their previous strategy session.

"I can see where that would pose a problem," John allowed, but it sounded like he wasn't going to make this easy. Like all good commanders, he had learned the value of making his subordinates squirm from time to time, it appeared.

Trevor took a deep breath and forged ahead. "Sir, I'd like your permission to join your community. Your Clan."

John looked at him for a moment then answered clearly, "No."

Trevor's heart sank. What was he going to do now?

"Don't look so glum, son," John went on, smiling in a friendly way. "The guys and I anticipated your situation and had a bit of a discussion about it after you and I spoke the other day. We may have a solution that will benefit not only Grizzly Cove, but your current Clan, as well. First, tell me what you plan to report back to Major Moore about us and how we performed in the most recent action."

"Sir, I've already made my preliminary report—just the brief after-action summary. The full rundown will go in tonight, and will include my personal impressions of you and your team. What I'd planned to tell the major is that you're a lot more battle ready than you let on. You may call yourselves retirees, but that's far from the truth, and I was going to propose the major seek an alliance with you and your men. He's been looking for top-notch groups like yours to work with ever since the Lords warned of increased enemy activity. I think your team here would be a good fit with our mission."

"Can you divulge your core mission?" Brody asked.

"To defeat evil wherever we find it." That was the core of everything the Wraiths did, and it was the measure they took of each proposed job before they agreed to take it on. The Wraiths didn't work for just anyone.

"Now that's a mission I can get behind," John agreed. "So, this is what we came up with. We'd like you to continue to act as a liaison between our team and your friends in Wyoming. We'll grant you residency here in the cove, and a sort of dual citizenship—something we've never tried before, but that seems appropriate in this particular case."

Trevor's hopes rose again. This proposal was better than anything he had expected.

He'd thought he'd have to give up his affiliation with his *friends in Wyoming*, as John put it, in order to make his home here in Grizzly Cove. In the normal course of business, he would have had to give up his Clan affiliation and try to form new bonds with the bears here, as a new member of their already established Clan. He would've been the low bear on the totem pole until he proved himself, which could take a long time.

The really special part about the group in Wyoming was that they weren't just bears. He had friends and coworkers across species lines. They had become true brothers in arms over the years they had fought side by side. They were his family, and it would've been difficult to sever those ties. But he would have done it for Beth. She was his mate. She was his family now, too.

The solution John proposed gave him hope that he wouldn't have to cut ties completely. Oh, there were a lot of details yet to be worked out, but Trevor would do everything in his power to make it happen. If Major Moore agreed, Trevor could have his cake and eat it too, in a manner of speaking.

"I'm going to formalize relations between

the Wraiths and my team, with the understanding that our theater of operations will be limited to this region, for the most part. On occasion, I can already foresee that some of my guys will be only too happy to join with the Wraiths for the odd mission here or there. Some of us—especially the ones that haven't found mates yet—still crave action in the real world from time to time. As you saw, we keep ourselves battle ready at all times. That seemed to be the wisest move, considering the unwanted attention we've unintentionally drawn from all sorts of evil opponents since day one." John seemed to think about that for a moment. "There have been some good things to come out of it, though. The alliance with Master Hiram is one, and Major Moore will have to be aware that Hiram has been investing in our town and making friends among my people. I've been approached by Samson Kinkaid, the lion Alpha, as well. So allying with Grizzly Cove brings with it connections to a few like-minded others, and possibly more in the future."

Trevor knew Moore would be pleased with both of the existing connections, though they'd have to do a bit more recon on the master vampire. Any future alliances would have to be vetted, but Trevor had great respect for the bears of Grizzly Cove and their cunning Alpha. They wouldn't get mixed up with anyone or anything that wasn't on the up and up.

"I don't think that will be a problem. The major has had me vetting possible allies for a while now, and Kinkaid is already on the cleared list. Master Hiram is on the list of possible allies, but we needed more intel before moving him over. Perhaps you can be of some assistance there."

"I'll do what I can," John agreed readily.

"Hiram's a good guy," Brody put in as John pushed some files around on his desk.

"Now then, all this is contingent on whether or not your mate wants to stay here," John continued. "I suppose she's about to inherit a mansion on Catalina Island and a small business empire. She might not want to stay."

"Negative on Catalina Island, sir. Beth is adamant about never going back there. The place holds some really bad memories for her. In fact, she's asked her mother to come here and meet Nansee and the pod, so you might be asked to shelter one more mermaid if Beth's mom agrees to come," Trevor told him. "However, there will be a lot to settle, and the possibility of needing to travel to take care of some of it. There's also the matter of Beth's stepfather having been involved in several highly illegal activities. I'd planned to ask the major if he could spare some men to act as backup for Beth and me when we have to travel to dismantle some of the criminal enterprises, but if any of your men want an adventure, I'd be pleased to have them at my side, any time."

John smiled. "I'll pass that along. I think you'll have a few takers, for sure."

Trevor rose, extending his hand to each of the men in turn. "Thanks for everything. I still have to talk to Beth about all of this, but I'll let you know. I appreciate that you planned this far ahead for us."

"I take care of my people, Trevor. That's a promise." John's words were solid, just like the man himself.

"I can see why your team made you Alpha." Trevor moved toward the door. "I always thought it was a bit odd—a bunch of independent bear shifters coming together here under an Alpha. That's not usually the way for our kind, as you well know. But I see why now."

John ducked his head a bit at the compliment, but said nothing as Trevor left his office. Trevor had things to do and people to talk to before he could lay out his plans before his mate. Goddess give him strength.

CHAPTER FOURTEEN

Trevor checked in with Jack by text message several times during the afternoon, to make sure everything was secure at the hotel. He had a few things to set up before he returned to his mate.

His mate. He savored that thought, hoping tonight would be the night that she'd accept him.

If she didn't, he'd spend the rest of his days trying to convince her. Eventually, she'd give in. He had to believe that.

But he didn't know where he stood yet. He'd been too cowardly to broach the subject with her to this point, so he wasn't even sure if she was leaning for or against them spending the rest of their lives together. He prayed to the Goddess that the odds were in his favor.

He wanted everything to be perfect tonight. He'd asked the ladies at the bakery—after things had settled down from the battle royale that had taken place earlier in the day—to set him up with a romantic picnic dinner for two. Normally, Trevor probably would've hit up Zak to cook something special, but the other man had his hands full at the jail. Nothing fancy would be coming out of the Cajun bear's kitchen today.

That was okay, though. The sisters who owned the bakery were supplying everyone with sandwiches, and it was all hands on deck in their little shop. They were more than happy to set up something nice for Trevor and Beth, once he asked.

The sisters gave him sly looks, and he realized his possible mating with Beth was probably one of the worst kept secrets in town. Only Beth, it seemed, didn't realize his intentions at this point. It was enough to make a bear growl.

But she'd know tonight. In no uncertain

terms. Trevor was going to lay his heart on the line for her and see what she did with it. He only hoped she would be gentle.

Trevor was used to battle and bleeding enemies, but putting his heart out there to be trampled on by the soft feet of his lover was something totally different. It was *a lot* scarier.

Beth was stiff from sitting so long by the end of the afternoon, but it had been worth it. She and Grace had begun to make inroads in tracking what Jonathan had been up to with all his shady businesses. They'd even managed to put an immediate stop to some of the worst things they had discovered. For example, they had been able to halt a huge shipment of illegal weapons before it ever left the warehouse. They'd also begun firing a lot of the unnecessary muscle her stepfather had employed.

The guards around the house on Catalina Island had been summarily sacked and replaced with some ex-Navy SEAL friends of Jack's, who lived somewhat near in the area and were willing to help out for a few months, until things settled down. Beth didn't want to leave her mother completely exposed in the big house, without any protection at all. The place was too much of a target. Jonathan had liked to live ostentatiously and had been conspicuous in every aspect of his consumption of Beth's wealth.

Thank the stars that was over.

She hadn't really had time to stop and think about what she had done, but oddly, taking Jonathan's life—the way it had gone down—didn't really bother her. It wasn't like she had murdered him in cold blood. She hadn't poisoned him, or lay in wait, or planned anything. No, he'd died as a direct result of his actions. Beth had been protecting her mate.

It was a shifter thing. Something mer, and all water shifters, understood. Protecting the mate was paramount. No one came before one's mate.

And Beth had been a member of the hunting party long enough to understand killing and death. She'd hunted to feed and protect the pod. She'd made her share of kills.

It had been hard at first, since she'd been raised mostly on land, and had never learned the ocean skills necessary for survival in the deeps. But her sisters in the hunting party had taught her the ropes. They'd been with her for her first kills and helped her learn and grow into a viable member of their team. She loved them—each and every one of them—for their patience and the care they had taken with her when she'd been so green. They were truly her sisters, and the fact that they'd been there to help her in her hour of greatest need would never be forgotten.

She'd thought moving to the cove had meant the end of her new family, but the battle early this morning had proven the exact opposite. It wasn't the end, but a new beginning, with a vastly expanded network of family members willing to help in times of crisis. She owed the bears a big apology for being such a pain in the ass since coming here. She realized now how patient they'd been with her and how gentle.

They could've torn into her at any time for some of the things she'd said and the actions she'd taken out of fear, but they'd held back. They'd given her time to figure things out. They'd acted like older siblings who knew, eventually, their recalcitrant little sister would get her shit together. She owed them all a debt of gratitude.

And now that she had her father's money at her disposal, she might begin to repay them in more tangible terms. The bears and her pod, both. Once she had a full picture of what was left after Jonathan's empire of evil had been dismantled, Beth planned to meet with Nansee and John to see how she could help the pod and the town with what was left.

The Catalina pod that her father had ruled was no more, but its legacy would live on in the newly-named Grizzly Cove pod. She knew her father would have been happy to finally see the wealth of his people go back to where it belonged.

"You know, judging by these bank balances," Grace had told her late in the afternoon, once they'd cracked the online banking portion of Jonathan's portfolio, "your stepfather actually made quite a bit of money for your trust fund. He doubled it, in fact."

"It's ill-gotten gains, in all likelihood," Beth had replied.

"The past can't be changed," Grace said, putting her hand over the back of Beth's hand where it rested on the desk. "What matters is what you do with it now."

Beth had agreed with the wisdom of her friend's words. Even now, as she closed up the makeshift office for the night and stretched her weary muscles, she was thinking of all the ways she could help the town and the people with all that cash. Grace was right. Beth would make it her mission to do good with the money her stepfather had made.

Grace and Jack took their leave only when Ezra returned to keep watch. Beth hadn't gotten much of a chance to talk to Ezra, and that didn't really change for the short time he sat with her until Trevor returned. The big bear bounty hunter was really a man of few words. Try as she might, she couldn't coax more than a few syllables out of him at a time.

Then again, he was probably just as tired as she was. Even more so. He'd been in the thick of battle and had been standing watch through the night before.

"When was the last time you slept?" she asked him now, as they sat together in the room that had been turned into her temporary office.

"I'll sleep when Trev gets back." That

was one of the longest sentences she'd managed to get out of him so far. She counted it a victory, of sorts.

"Did you get hurt during the fight?" She had the sneaking suspicion the big bear wouldn't admit to pain, but she couldn't help asking.

To that question, he only shrugged. Hmm. She was right. Ezra wasn't one to make a fuss about a little blood. Obstinate man.

"Did the doctor at least take a look at you?" She tried again.

"What for?" He shrugged again, and she thought she detected a bit of a wince, but she couldn't be positive. "I'm fine."

"Look, Ezra. I want to thank you for coming all this way to help me and Trevor. I can see you're a true friend to him, and it means a lot to me that you were willing to forego the enormous bounty Jonathan had put on my head and actually help me." She waited, but that didn't even rate a single syllable in reply. Maybe her next words would elicit a real response. "I want to pay you."

He seemed to perk up, but the expression on his face appeared a bit insulted, if she was any judge. Of course, he might just have indigestion for all she knew. The man was hard to read.

"I mean…like…give you a job," she tried to clarify. "If you want it. As you can see, I've got a lot of work ahead of me to close down all of Jonathan's illegal operations." She gestured to the mountain of paper she'd generated today that sat on the desk behind her. "I could use some help. Help I can trust."

Now, he looked more interested.

"What would you want me to do?"

Well. Seven whole words, but still all single syllables. Still, it was a longer sentence, as Ezra's sentences went, so she'd take it.

"Troubleshooter," she answered immediately, having thought this through during the afternoon when she looked at evidence of some of the more complex operations and realized shutting them down couldn't be done remotely. "Take this for example." She reached behind her for a sheaf of papers. "This business looks legit on the outside, but Jonathan didn't have a single legitimate bone in his body. There's something fishy going on here, but it would require boots on the ground—to borrow one of Trevor's phrases—to figure out what's really going on and how to put an end to it."

She handed the newly created paper file over to Ezra and paused while he flipped through it. He frowned a few times, grimaced once, but otherwise seemed interested in what she'd uncovered so far. He'd be perfect to infiltrate some of the seamier businesses and straighten them out. He had killer instinct and a rough appearance, but she'd learned a lot about him over the past hours, and she knew for certain he was one of the good guys. He'd be perfect for the job she had in mind.

At length, he sat back and closed the file. "I'm in."

Trevor returned to the hotel just after dark to find Beth and Ezra deep in conversation over a pile of thick folders. They were still in the room he'd commandeered that morning to use as an office, and while Beth was doing most of the talking, Trevor was suitably impressed with how much Ezra was contributing to the conversation.

Somehow, his cunning little mate had

found a way to draw out the most taciturn of Trevor's friends. He had to smile, seeing them bent over the file, pointing out some sort of trail in what looked like a bank ledger. They were so engrossed in the work that Beth didn't even realize Trevor had returned.

Ezra looked up and gave him the all clear signal, meaning Ezra had probably realized the moment Trevor had entered the building. Good man. Ezra might be a bear, but he was better than any watchdog on the planet at sensing trouble. If he was calm, Trevor knew it was safe. For now, at least.

"I brought dinner," Trevor said, stepping into the temporary office. Only then did Beth look up, her face transformed by a bright smile when she saw him that made the whole hellish day worthwhile.

"Great. I'm starved," she replied, standing and stretching her back. Poor baby had been sitting at that desk all day from the reports he'd received.

Trevor might've been running around town and making long-distance calls all day, but he'd kept up with his woman through the men who had been guarding her. First Jack and then Ezra had been sending him periodic updates via text message, unbeknownst to Beth.

Trevor hoisted two big brown paper shopping bags in the air. One was slightly larger, having been packed for two, but the other one held enough for a hungry shifter. The gals at the bakery had set up an assembly line of sorts, packing bags just like this to take out to the guys on guard duty, since the troops were spread a bit thin after the action of the morning.

"Courtesy of the Grizzly Cove bakery," Trevor said as he handed the bag to Ezra. "Want to eat with us? You two looked like you were deep in discussions." Trevor wasn't being nosy, but he had to admit to being intrigued about what Ezra and Beth could have possibly been so engrossed in.

Ezra shook his head as he stood. "Beth will tell you," he said with characteristic brevity. "I stand watch for another hour, then I'm off for six." It went without saying that he'd only be next door if he was needed, but Ezra wasn't superman. He had to sleep sometime, and he'd fought hard that morning, alongside the others, then spent the afternoon sorting out bounty hunters from hired goons with the sheriff's department. He'd put in a full day, and then some.

"Who's on duty after you?" Trevor asked, knowing they wouldn't be left unguarded with all the miscreants still in town, even if they were either in the clinic or the jail. Or in the morgue.

"Big John said he'd take care of it," Ezra answered. They both knew that, if John said a thing would be done, by golly, it would be done. Nothing got past the best strategic mind Delta Force had even known.

"Fair enough." Trevor turned his focus to his mate. "Are you about ready to head back to our room?" He'd caught her mid-yawn and tried not to grin.

"Oh, yeah. I'm done with this for the day. Let's go." She stood and moved toward the door, but paused on the way as she passed Ezra.

"Thanks for everything," she said with a fond smile. "I'm glad you accepted my offer."

"Me, too, boss lady." Ezra actually grinned at her, and Trevor grew even more intrigued.

He'd never known stoic Ezra to take to someone so quickly. Hell, he'd known the guy for five years before he'd ever gotten more than three words out of the man. Somehow, Trevor's sweet mate had not only gotten Ezra to talk to her, but to agree to her mysterious offer? Would wonders never cease?

Trevor tried not to laugh as he followed his mate out of the room. Ezra trailed after, locking the door behind them. The paperwork would keep until tomorrow.

Ezra checked Trevor's room while he held back with Beth, just as a precaution. When Ezra emerged and gave the thumbs up, Trevor escorted Beth inside, waiting to make sure Ezra was safe in his own room before shutting and locking the door.

"Alone at last," he said, turning to find Beth grinning as she attacked the big bag of sandwiches and pastries. "So, are you going to tell me what kind of offer you made to Ezra while I was otherwise engaged? Should I be jealous?" He kept his tone light, his words teasing.

He didn't think she'd turn to another man, but their relationship was still so new and so unsure. Trevor desperately wanted her to confirm he was her one and only mate, but he was afraid. Yep. Trevor

Williams, Special Operator and badass mercenary bear, was afraid the woman of his dreams would reject him.

"Jealous? Nope. Not unless you wanted the job as troubleshooter for my inherited business holdings," she responded in the same vein, already placing wrapped sandwiches out for both of them.

He moved closer to the small table at the far end of the room. She'd set the places with the plastic knives, forks and spoons that had been packed with the sandwiches, and set cups and plates down for each of them. He liked the way she made even paper plates and plastic utensils seem special. Homey. Domestic. Like they were already a mated pair.

"You offered him a job?" Now, Trevor was *really* impressed.

Ezra was the kind of bear that always roamed alone. The bounty hunter lifestyle had suited him to a T. Going place to place on his Harley, hunting fugitives, never really settling anywhere. That was the life Ezra's restless bear demanded.

Trevor knew there were reasons for that. Dark reasons. Deep scars that had made Ezra the man he'd become.

If Ezra was ready to take a steadier job, that was really something. Of course, it was hard to say no to Beth. Trevor knew that well enough. But still, this was big news and a major improvement for the bear Trevor had feared would never change from his lonely, nomadic ways.

"Well, it became clear as I was looking through the various accounts and businesses today that a lot of these things need to be handled in person. After everything we've been through in such a short time, I trust Ezra to be on the right side of things. He proved himself when he didn't come after me for the price on my head. I trust him." She set a wrapped sandwich before Trevor as they both sat at the small table. "And I don't necessarily have the skills or the desire to travel all over the place, rooting out the bad guys and shutting down criminal enterprises. I think Ezra does. He looks just rough enough to be able to infiltrate where the bad guys are and then learn what he needs to shut them down."

"It's a genius idea, honey." Trevor was proud of his clever mate.

She blushed so prettily, it was all he could do to stop himself from leaning over the table to kiss her. But he had to be patient. Eat first. Pounce on her after. That was the plan, such as it was.

"Honestly, he strikes me as a lonely soul," Beth said contemplatively. "I don't think bounty hunting is a very stable sort of profession. I get that the hunting part probably satisfies his inner predator, but not having a home territory or Clan… That's got to be rough. This might give him some…for lack of a better word…roots." She took a drink of her water before continuing. "I want him to feel connected to us. To our people, here in Grizzly Cove. Maybe if he knew he was welcome, he might someday think of this as a place to return to. I take it the other bears here liked what they saw of him, right? He seems to have fit right in with the others."

"Very observant," Trevor agreed. "He impressed the Alpha and his XO. I'm pretty sure they'd accept him into the community if he asked, but I'll be honest. It'll take a lot to get Ezra to ask. He's a man with baggage, and that won't be gotten rid of that easily." Trevor shook his head. "But I'm really glad you've taken him under your wing. The job with you—and the connections—will be good for him. You're right when you say he needs roots. He's been drifting a long time."

"He really is a good friend to you, isn't he?" she asked, watching him with a gentle expression.

"Ezra is more like a brother to me than even he knows." Trevor couldn't really say more than that. Ezra was special. It was as simple as that.

"Then, I'm doubly glad he accepted the job," Beth replied after a moment. Her smile was soft as she returned to her food. She'd been through an awful lot that day, and yet, she'd shown the strength he'd known she'd possessed, but hadn't fully realized.

Dinner was pleasant enough and they talked of mostly benign stuff. All the while, Beth felt the weight of her need to claim him as her mate sitting between them. Was he feeling the same pull or was she deluding herself?

As they lingered over dessert, the conversation fell into a lull. It had a been a long, difficult, momentous, life-altering day.

"Beth…" Trevor's uncharacteristically hesitant tone made her look up at him. "Are you really okay with what went down this morning?"

She knew what he meant. He was talking about her trident, and how it had snuffed the life out of her nemesis. The evil bastard that had called himself her stepfather. She couldn't really feel remorse for ridding the world of such a man, though she knew her reaction was probably a little strange—or would seem that way to Trevor.

"Although I've never killed someone before, I'm good with what happened, I think," she answered honestly, really thinking about her words. "I guess the predator in me recognized Jonathan as the shark that shared his soul more than a man. He lived very close to the edge. He couldn't always control his shifts, which is why he had to live on the water with a private beach. When he lost his temper...or really, anytime at all...he would shift into his animal form uncontrollably. It wasn't uncommon to see him running for the surf, ripping out of his hand-tailored suits." She shook her head at the memory. She hadn't really thought about these things in a very long time.

"If he was that out of control of his beast, he had to have been close to feral," Trevor observed, his brows drawing together in concern.

"Now that I look back on it, I think that was the case. He put on a good show for the few humans he dealt with, but he was all shark, pretty much all the time." It was startling to realize that she'd lived with such a monster for so long. "When I joined Nansee's pod, I knew next to nothing about how to be mer. I couldn't hunt. I'd never even fished in my human form. I didn't know how to kill or dress a catch. I was like a child. But the girls in my hunting party taught me what I needed to know, and I became one of the best hunters in the group."

She felt the need to explain her thoughts, though she would never justify her actions to anyone else. Only Trevor. He needed to know where she was coming from.

"So, killing Jonathan was like killing a shark in the ocean?" he asked.

Beth shrugged. "Not exactly, but there are parallels. I didn't hunt him, of course. And that's probably why my human half is okay with the way everything happened this morning. It wasn't quite self-defense, but I was protecting your back and defending myself in the process. It's not like I planned it. It just happened. And my mer side was cool about it. My inner predator recognized the need to take out the two-legged shark for the safety of my people—which includes you, Trevor."

She said that last bit quietly, wondering what he'd make of her words. Would he understand that she was claiming him? That her mer half saw him as hers?

"That's good, Beth," he said, after some hesitation. "That's really good."

"Which part?" she challenged.

"The part where you called me one of your people?" He gave her a smile as he looked at her, questions in his eyes that she was starting to feel more confident about answering.

"Well, you are. I mean, you're not just *one* of the people I care about…" Now or never, she told herself, taking a deep breath before continuing. "You're *the* person I care about."

"That sounds serious," he told her, moving around the table to kneel before her chair. He took her hands in his in a move that was so romantic she thought her heart might burst. "Would it be okay to say that you're the person I care about too?"

She nodded, her breath caught in her

throat as their gazes met and held. He looked so earnest. So serious. So...hopeful. That expression gave her hope, as well.

"Would it be okay to say that you're my mate, Beth?" he whispered, drawing closer to her as she heard words she thought she might never hear.

Her soul filled with joy as she slid out of the chair and wrapped her arms around him. They sat together, right there on the floor, clinging to each other.

"Yes, Trevor," she whispered near his ear as she hugged him tight. "Because you're my mate too."

CHAPTER FIFTEEN

Trevor was glad he was already on the floor, because after hearing Beth call him her mate, he knew his knees wouldn't support him. He held her close, reveling in the moment. He'd been half-afraid most of his life that this day would never come.

Now that it was here, he wanted to enjoy the moment...and all the moments to come. He'd found his mate, and nothing would ever be the same again. From now on, it would be his honor and privilege to look out for not just himself but her, as well. They were a pair now. A team. A partnership that superseded every other commitment in his life.

They would grow into it. Although shifters often knew when they met the person destined to be their life partner, the relationship grew and matured over time. The attraction was instant, and potent as hell, but the path to true understanding was a journey they would undertake together...for the rest of their lives.

It promised to be amazing.

And it all started right here. Right now.

Trevor pushed off from the floor, lifting Beth in his arms and depositing her on the nearby bed. She smiled at him as he set her down, her fingers tangling in his shirt and pulling him down toward her. She matched her lips to his in a kiss that was both exhilarating and new. She was claiming him as much as he was her. A partnership of equals.

They didn't speak for long moments while their kiss went on and on. Clothes got in the way, and he made them disappear. He wasn't conscious of his movements, only that he had to get skin to skin with his mate as quickly as possible.

His mate! She'd said it. She felt it, too, thank the Goddess.

When he had them both naked, skin to skin, he lay next to her on the wide bed, leaning over on his side so he could kiss her. He wanted to take this slow. After all, they'd just mutually acknowledged something that would change their lives forever. There was just one little thing left to put out there. He lifted his head and looked deep into her eyes.

"Just so you know... I love you, Beth."

When Trevor declared his love so straightforward and simply, it took her breath away. Tears quickly welled behind her eyes. Tears of a happiness so profound, she wasn't sure how to deal with it. The only thing she could think of was to return his honesty with her own.

Throwing her arms around his neck, she let the emotion of the moment rule.

"I love you, too, Trevor." She placed kisses all over his face, wherever she could reach. "So much."

His laughter was rich and genuine, and it touched her deeply. She felt the same bubbling joy. It was a happiness she thought she might never find, and now, here she was, with her one true mate. How had she been so blessed?

They made love slowly, cherishing every moment. At least, that's the way it felt to Beth. Trevor had undressed her with the impatience that had been characteristic of their moments of passion up to this point, but with the declaration of love, it felt like, suddenly, they had time. Or maybe it was the resolution of Beth's problems with Jonathan that had changed things.

Beth was much more secure now, and Trevor had played a major role in making that happen. He'd given her room to breathe by protecting her with love and care. He hadn't stifled her in any way, and ultimately, he'd been okay with the way things had ended.

Trevor hadn't seemed at all negative about the way she'd taken the killing shot at Jonathan when he'd been poised to injure or kill Trevor. There was no pride, no one-upmanship, no jealousy. Only concern that she was emotionally okay after the ordeal.

Trevor's concern had been for her throughout. His ego didn't interfere with their relationship. That was important to her because she'd grown up watching Jonathan—who was nothing but ego—destroy her mother's spirit with his overbearing ways.

She loved the way Trevor's strong hands felt against her most sensitive skin. He cupped her breasts in both hands as he kissed his way down her neck. Lifting her nipples toward his mouth, he spent time making sure he didn't miss one millimeter of excited flesh in his mission to tease every part of her body.

When he had her sighing in pleasure, he moved on...slowly. Trevor seemed to be making a concentrated effort to drive her out of her ever-loving mind. It was delicious torture. And when he settled between her thighs and spread her wide, she sucked in a sharp breath as his tongue zeroed in on her clit.

"Trev!" she gasped, the sensations his tongue evoked as he used it in ways she'd never dared dream about on her most sensitive flesh making her squirm.

She could feel his lips smile against her, and that, too, was one of the most erotic moments of her life to date. Everything about Trevor was new and exciting, strange and completely fascinating.

He kissed his way back up her body, pausing here and there to whisper words of love and praise. When he reached her lips again, she sighed into his kiss as he rose over her body. He joined them together simply. Slowly. As if they had all the time in the world.

And they did. She realized they had the rest of their lives to share this incredible intimacy. All those days to learn each other and every night to spend in each other's arms. The future—for the first time ever—looked bright, indeed.

Trevor made love to her gently, but with increasing vigor. He altered their positions multiple times, bringing her to climax over and over again before allowing her that big final orgasm in which he joined her, whispering her name and all sorts of exciting words into her ear as he thrust from behind. Somehow, they'd ended up doggy style, but she wasn't complaining.

Trevor was proving to be a very thorough and inventive lover, and she had a lot to learn. She already knew she would enjoy each and every lesson.

Later, as they lay together in the aftermath, Trevor realized he still had a few things to clear up with Beth. He'd laid all the groundwork. Now, he needed to tell her what he'd done and make it clear to her that she didn't have to give up her friends in the pod for him.

"You know, I had a talk with Big John today." He broached the subject cautiously, not sure how to proceed. He'd take his cues from her responses.

She turned toward him on the bed, putting her hand across his chest and her head on his shoulder. He felt the warmth of affection blossom in his heart anew. Life with her was going to be glorious.

He just had to make sure she realized she had options. He'd spent a lot of time that afternoon trying to set things up. Now, he just had to see which way she wanted to go.

"I also talked to my commanding officer, Major Moore, back in Wyoming."

"Really?" She yawned and snuggled closer. He forged ahead, figuring, if she fell asleep, at least he could use this as a practice run for when she woke up.

"I live there, you know. In Wyoming. But I have a sense that it wouldn't be the ideal place for you. Any water we have is frozen a good part of the year. Of course, the skiing is great, but I get the idea you need the ocean."

"Mm-hmm," she agreed, nodding faintly against his chest.

"So, I asked John if I could join the guys here in Grizzly Cove, since this is where your pod is based for now, but he came up with what I think is an even better solution." He wasn't sure if she was still listening, but he kept talking, anyway. "Major Moore and Big John have agreed to grant me a unique sort of dual-citizenship. I'm still part of the Wraiths, and I can keep my cabin on the mountain in Wyoming for now, but we can live here in Grizzly Cove. Or we can go wherever else you want. I figure you'd like the coast. California? Or Oregon? Wherever you like."

"I like it here," she replied, proving she'd been listening all along. She rose up to meet his gaze. "And I love it that you put so much thought into this." She leaned down to kiss him. "Thank you, my love." She kissed him again. "But you should know, I would've gone anywhere as long as I'm with you. If you really want to stay with your friends in Wyoming, I'm okay with that. We'll figure it out. And I really would like to learn how to ski, sometime." She kissed him a little longer this time.

It meant the world to him that she'd been willing to give up the ocean to be with him, but he'd arranged it so she wouldn't have to. They were both thinking of each other, which meant their relationship was off to a really good start. Love would see them through whatever issues might arise.

*

They held a birthday party for Beth a few days later, attended by all their friends. It was really a combination birthday and mating celebration. They'd gone public—to the surprise of absolutely no one in Grizzly Cove—the day after the battle, to the good wishes of all their friends.

Now that she was of legal age to inherit the property that had been left in trust for her, she was able to begin legal proceedings to fully deconstruct what Jonathan had built. The mated lawyer pair that called Grizzly Cove home—Tom and his mate, Ashley—had already begun writing up the necessary documents. There would be plenty of work for the lawyers and for Trevor, Beth and the team she was building, starting with Ezra.

It might take months—possibly even

years—but they'd fix what Jonathan had broken. It was something Beth had vowed to do, regardless of how long it took. She'd also resolved to help her mother and had already sent a shifter psychologist to talk with her mother at the big house on Catalina Island. The preliminary report had confirmed Beth's suspicions, without breaching patient confidentiality, that Beth's mother had faced years of abuse, both physical and psychological. It was going to take time for her mother to heal, but at least she had it now. Time and space away from Jonathan and his goons.

Maybe, someday, Beth's mother would come visit, or maybe even choose to stay in Grizzly Cove, but for now, she had her own demons to put to rest. Beth trusted the people she'd put in place to help her mother with Trevor's help. The psychologist was someone he knew and who had worked with civilian victims of violence many times. Major Moore had a number of qualified people like that on call because he was one of the good guys, and he didn't like to leave a trail of traumatized people in his wake.

When the Wraiths rescued someone, they truly rescued them—in every sense of the word.

That was certainly true in Beth's case. Trevor had come into her life and rescued her from a future without him in it. A future in which she would have continued to be afraid of every little change.

Come to think of it, she probably would've been captured by one of those bounty hunters and sent back to Jonathan. That was no future at all, as far as she was concerned.

Instead, with Trevor in her life, Beth had finally come into her own. The problem with her stepfather had come to a head and been dealt with once and for all. Her inner predator had finally made peace with her previously wimpy human half, and not only was she in better harmony with herself, but she was in better harmony with all those around her who had put up with her whining for so very long.

Beth was well and truly rescued, and Trevor continued to be a source of love and delight in her life as they worked through the residual issues left by Jonathan's actions. She was surrounded by friends and the man she loved more than life itself, celebrating a birthday she almost didn't live to see, in a place she intended to call home for the foreseeable future.

Life couldn't get much better than this.

Just as she had that thought, Trevor returned to her side and took her into her arms.

"I stand corrected," she whispered as he swept her into a slow dance on the beach where they'd set up party lights and had music playing. Her party was for land and sea shifters alike and was taking place in a venue both groups could easily enjoy.

"What's that, my love?" Trevor whispered near her ear as they swayed to the music.

"I was just thinking things couldn't get any better, and then, you took me into your arms. You proved me wrong. It did get better—just because you're here." She reached up and kissed him gently. "I love you, my mate."

"I love you too."

They danced the night away under the stars, surrounded by friends in a place of peace and harmony. Grizzly Cove had made Beth's dreams—even the ones she hadn't really dared to dream—come true.

ABOUT THE AUTHOR

Bianca D'Arc has run a laboratory, climbed the corporate ladder in the shark-infested streets of lower Manhattan, studied and taught martial arts, and earned the right to put a whole bunch of letters after her name, but she's always enjoyed writing more than any of her other pursuits. She grew up and still lives on Long Island, where she keeps busy with an extensive garden, several aquariums full of very demanding fish, and writing her favorite genres of paranormal, fantasy and sci-fi romance.

Bianca loves to hear from readers and can be reached via Facebook (BiancaDArcAuthor) or through the various links on her website.

WELCOME TO THE D'ARC SIDE…
WWW.BIANCADARC.COM

OTHER BOOKS
BY BIANCA D'ARC

Paranormal Romance

Brotherhood of Blood
One & Only
Rare Vintage
Phantom Desires
Sweeter Than Wine
Forever Valentine
Wolf Hills*
Wolf Quest

Tales of the Were
Lords of the Were
Inferno
Rocky
Slade

Tales of the Were ~ Redstone Clan
The Purrfect Stranger
Grif
Red
Magnus
Bobcat
Matt

Tales of the Were ~ String of Fate
Cat's Cradle
King's Throne
Jacob's Ladder
Her Warriors

Tales of the Were ~ Grizzly Cove
All About the Bear
Mating Dance
Night Shift
Alpha Bear
Saving Grace
Bearliest Catch
The Bear's Healing Touch
The Luck of the Shifters
Badass Bear

Guardians of the Dark
Half Past Dead
Once Bitten, Twice Dead
A Darker Shade of Dead
The Beast Within
Dead Alert

Gifts of the Ancients: Warrior's Heart

Epic Fantasy Erotic Romance

Dragon Knights
Maiden Flight*
The Dragon Healer
Border Lair
Master at Arms
The Ice Dragon**
Prince of Spies***
Wings of Change
FireDrake
Dragon Storm
Keeper of the Flame
Hidden Dragons
The Sea Captain's Daughter Trilogy
Book 1: Sea Dragon
Book 2: Dragon Fire
Book 3: Dragon Mates

Science Fiction Romance

StarLords
Hidden Talent
Talent For Trouble
Shy Talent

Jit'Suku Chronicles ~ Arcana
King of Swords
King of Cups
King of Clubs
King of Stars
End of the Line
Diva

Jit'Suku Chronicles ~ Sons of Amber
Angel in the Badlands
Master of Her Heart

Futuristic Erotic Romance

Resonance Mates
Hara's Legacy**
Davin's Quest
Jaci's Experiment
Grady's Awakening
Harry's Sacrifice

* RT Book Reviews Awards Nominee
** EPPIE Award Winner
*** CAPA Award Winner

WWW.BIANCADARC.COM

Made in the USA
San Bernardino, CA
16 June 2017